4. Feb 2012 ... 1 4 FEB 2012

CAN
01/12

2 8 FEB 2012

3 0 JUN 2012

Books should be returned or renewed by the last date
above. Renew by phone **08458 247 200** or online
www.kent.gov.uk/libs

Libraries & Archives

The Blue Book

Christopher Bowden

LANGTON & WOOD

Reprinted 2010

Distributed by Gardners Books, 1 Whittle Drive, Eastbourne,
East Sussex, BN23 6QH
Tel: +44(0)1323 521555 | Fax: +44(0)1323 521666

British Library Cataloguing in Publication Data
A catalogue record for this book is available from the
British Library.

ISBN 978-0-9555067-0-3

Typeset by Amolibros, Milverton, Somerset
This book production has been managed by Amolibros
Printed and bound by T J International Ltd, Padstow, Cornwall, UK

Lines from 'The Waste Land' from *The Waste Land and Other Poems* by T S Eliot are used by kind permission of Faber and Faber Ltd.

Prologue

*H*ugh Mullion walked back home from the station that evening for the last time. He and his partner, Kate Roberts, were moving from this part of south London in the morning. As he made his way down the parade flanked by Bin Ends and the betting shop, Hugh paused to look in the window of Peter's Antiques. A copper warming pan on the wall gleamed quietly in the light of a small table lamp. The dappled rocking horse in the corner appeared to rock gently back and forth, as if pushed by an invisible hand. The horse's eyes betrayed a hint of sadness. Hugh sighed and thought of the hours he had spent there and at Toad Books next door. The bookshop was in darkness now, the boxes in which he used to rummage put away for another day. You never knew what you were going to find. Perhaps if he had known what he would find under the polythene, and where it would lead, that wet autumn Saturday of the previous year, he would have been more circumspect. But there was no putting the clock back. Hugh thought yet again of those events as he carried on down the parade and turned the corner into Dogberry Road.

Part One

Toad Books – second-hand and antiquarian books bought and sold; collections purchased – occupied the premises of a former draper and haberdasher. A few local residents could still remember the shop as it used to be: the peeling brown paint, the yellowing bolts of cloth, the grubby doilies in the window. At the time of the transformation a dozen or so years ago, Toad Books had been one of three such bookshops in the area. Now it was the sole survivor.

Hugh stumbled over the threshold and extricated the sleeve of his coat from the door handle. His dark brown hair was damp from the rain. He greeted Marjorie, the long-suffering assistant of the proprietor, Anthony Buffo, and went over to the grey parrot skulking on the top of an open cage, which rested on an upturned dustbin.

"Good morning, Charlie," said Hugh.

"Bugger off," said Charlie, inspecting the apple core he held in his foot.

"Charlie's not in the best of humour this morning."

"He's always unsettled when Mr Buffo's been away," said Marjorie. "New York again. Only got back this morning. You know how attached to each other they are." She toyed with one of the textured daisies decorating her dark blue crew neck sweater. "And on top of that there was the Vivaldi on the radio. It was much too frenetic for Charlie. He's more of a Cole Porter bird. He likes to sing along. It came on completely without warning. I don't know why they play *Primavera* at this time of year, I really don't. It's all wrong. They should stick to...*Autumn*...for the next few months."

"Well, on that basis you'd have to wait a year to hear the whole of *The Four Seasons*," said Hugh. He laid a book on the pine table that served as Marjorie's desk. "I found this outside but it's only Volume II. Do you have Volume I secreted somewhere?"

Marjorie picked up the book and brought the spine into focus. "*The Portrait of a Lady*," she read, a trifle ponderously. "Henry James. You could try Fiction or Literature or Classics. That accounts for most of that sort of thing. Unless, of course, it's very small, in which case it'll be with the Pocket Books in the bookcase under the window by Charlie. Or illustrated, in which case it'll be over there next to the Folio Society. Or a Modern First Edition. They're in the cabinet behind me."

"I'll see if I can root it out."

As Hugh drifted towards J on the Literature shelves, a man with a pointed nose, a gloomy expression and a brown raincoat came into the bookshop. "I don't suppose you've got it," he said to Marjorie. "It's quite old. Destroyed in the Blitz, I shouldn't wonder. A lot of books were. It's about newts and salamanders. I'll look at Natural History, if I may. Not much chance, though. That parrot's made rather a mess. Seeds and suchlike on the carpet. I daresay it'll attract mice. I'd keep a cat if I were you."

"We hoover up after Charlie every day," said Anthony Buffo, coming downstairs with a large box marked 'Baked Beans'. He placed the box on the floor beside several others and mopped his moist and shining brow with a crumpled silk handkerchief. A bead of perspiration still glistened above his small black moustache. His faintly olive skin suggested a touch of the Mediterranean lurking somewhere in the background.

Anthony went over to Charlie's cage, produced a champagne cork from the pocket of his trousers, and offered it to the delighted bird.

"Charlie's looking forward to the book fair tomorrow," he said to Hugh, who was now immersed in Classics, balancing with one foot on the bottom rung of a small stepladder. "He never misses a fair and the customers love him. A fellow of infinite jest and a great lover of cardboard boxes. He'll destroy anything if you let him."

"I deplore frivolity in a bird," said the man with the pointed nose as he made his way to the door. "I take a serious view of life. Pets should be kept in their place. Nothing on newts or salamanders, as I expected. Looks like the rain's set in."

*

Hugh was coming away from Classics as Anthony reappeared with a box of Rupert annuals.

"I haven't managed to find Volume I of this," he said, handing Anthony the dark blue book he had shown Marjorie.

"No, you won't. It was just an odd volume in the bottom of a box of books I got at the auction. That's why I put it outside. Do you still want it?"

"I might as well for 50p. The other one may turn up. And I'll have this Trollope for Kate, if I may."

"Certainly. Marjorie will do the biz."

Marjorie took two pens from the tobacco jar on the table. With the black one she wrote in a large ledger the titles of the two books and the sums involved. With the red one she added the total underneath. "That's £3.25, please, Mr Mullet."

"It's Mullion, but please call me Hugh," he said through gritted teeth. They went through this performance every time.

On his way out of the bookshop Hugh brushed past a few late geraniums in the large terracotta pot that guarded the doorway. The sun was shining brightly in a clear blue sky.

The police were just leaving as Kate came home from the Centre for Natural Medicine, a converted piano factory where she practised as a homeopath. Slim, but not slight, she was carrying a black remedy case and a sturdy bag containing her Materia Medica and Kent's Repertory, the tools of her trade. As Kate approached the late Victorian terraced house that was number 40 Dogberry Road she saw Hugh loitering palely by the maroon front door. He was alone.

"Oh, not again," said Kate. "What was it this time? Did you forget the code?"

"Not as such. I pressed the right numbers but one didn't take. Then there was a horrible noise. When the alarm company rang I couldn't remember the password. I knew it was Iris or Isis or Osiris or something like that."

"It's Ibis. Just like it was last time and the time before. We'll get another rude letter. This road's impossible."

Kate closed the wooden gate behind her. "I had to park right at the other end by the pub."

"The King's Head?"

"It changed its name to O'Malley's two years ago, Hugh. That's when they painted it emerald green. And that removal van doesn't help. It's taking up enough room for three cars." Kate was pointing at the bright yellow pantechnicon of Messrs Tumbril and Robinson, familiar in South Coast towns for over half a century but rarely seen in this part of the world.

"I don't suppose it'll be there much longer," said Hugh. "They've made good progress with their tea chests."

As he spoke, two men were struggling with a king size bed. "Down a bit at your end, Dave. Tilt it and round. That's it."

"I don't know what Gordon West wants with a bed that size," said Hugh. "It's just him, I gather."

"Gordon West?"

"He's the one moving in to number 42. He introduced himself when he came out to see what the noise was a few minutes ago."

"He can only be an improvement on those Gurnings and their screaming brat."

"Eleanor was rather nice when she was quiet," said Hugh. "I wouldn't mind…"

"Could you take this bag?" said Kate. "The books weigh a ton. The sooner I get a laptop the better."

"Christ! They *are* heavy. Coffee?"

*

Hugh held two striped mugs in one hand and a packet of biscuits in the other. He put them all on the kitchen table. "So how was the world of complementary medicine this morning?" he asked, dunking a bourbon into his coffee. "A constant succession of diseases, maladies and distressing ailments?" Beneath the veneer of gentle mockery Hugh wasn't quite sure whether he believed in all this alternative stuff or not.

"You may laugh. A lot of people take homeopathy seriously, which is just as well for me. Even Dickens and Thackeray took the plunge. That ought to appeal to you. And what about the Royal Family?"

"I'm a firm believer in the Monarchy myself," said Hugh, reaching for a second bourbon. "A pillar of the Constitution and a great tourist attraction."

"Right. No more biscuits," said Kate. Ignoring Hugh's protests, she confiscated the packet and put it in the drawer of the kitchen table. "Wanda at reception completely screwed up the appointments so I was running miles behind. And then Clare and Linda popped in for a chat afterwards."

"Remind me which of the dark arts they practise."

Kate did not rise to the bait. "Clare does shiatsu, Linda does acupuncture. At least they like my hair."

"So do I. It just takes a bit of getting used to. Henna, isn't it?"

"Yeah. Hand me that bag. I want to see if there's a remedy for technophobia and an inability to deal with the modern world. The twenty-first century isn't really your thing, is it?"

"I thought you weren't supposed to treat your own family."

"Not quite family."

"Well, as good as. 'We've been together now for...' What is it? Five years? Six?"

"Four, actually. This repertory's falling apart."

"Your homeopathy things always do. Why are so many printed in India on such lousy paper? I got you a book, by the way. Another Trollope." Hugh removed the book from the modest pile on the dresser next to a large ceramic pumpkin. "*The Vicar of Bullhampton*."

"Thanks," said Kate, glancing at the mawkish picture on the front cover and at the blurb on the back. "I don't know this one. What else did you get?" Without waiting for an answer she stretched over and picked up the remaining book. "*The Portrait of a Lady*. Since when did you read Henry James?"

"I don't. Or haven't, anyway. I just liked the feel of it. Rather smart with its gilt lettering and decoration against the blue, don't you think?"

"This is Volume II. Where's the other one?"

"I don't know. They only had this one," Hugh said plaintively.

"Honestly. What's the use of that?" Kate opened the book. "It starts at Chapter twenty-eight," she said, decoding the roman numerals. " 'On the morrow'," she read, " 'in the evening, Lord Warburton went again to see his friends at their hotel, and at this establishment he learned that they had gone to the opera.' I suppose it might make sense if you'd read the previous twenty-seven chapters. I wonder what happened to Dorothy Russell?"

"Who is Dorothy Russell?"

"A previous owner, I should think. Here, look."

Hugh read on the flyleaf a small neat inscription in blue-black ink:

Dorothy Russell
St Helen's
May 1944.

"Merseyside during the Second World War," he said. "Heaven knows how it ended up in a bookshop in south London. This edition was published in 1921 so it had a life well before Dorothy. Twenty-three years. Only six less than you, Kate."

Hugh flicked through the pages of the book. "Hello. What's this?" He removed a small piece of paper, tissue-thin, and unfolded it. There was something written on it. 'D. Fear death by water.' How odd. I wonder what it means."

"Same writing as the inscription," said Kate. " 'Fear death by water.' 'Fear death by water'," she repeated more slowly. "That rings a bell."

"Probably a warning to some unfortunate wartime pilot."

"Looks like he never got it then. Hang on. Just a minute. I've had a thought." Kate got up from the table and ran upstairs to the spare bedroom, which doubled as a study and dumping ground for things that had no homes elsewhere. She opened the glass-fronted bookcase that Hugh had got cheap from Peter's Antiques in the parade, ran her eye along the second shelf and removed a book. She opened it and flipped the pages backwards and forwards, briefly distracted by familiar lines and the memory of half-forgotten voices. She found what she wanted and went back to the kitchen.

"Here we are. Look. It's from *The Waste Land*. Blah, blah, blah: '…I do not find the Hanged Man. Fear death by water.' How strange. I wonder what it means. I don't think there were too many Phoenician sailors on Merseyside, drowned or otherwise."

"But Madame Sosostris could have done with a good remedy for her cold."

"You are learning. There's hope for you yet. Where's the cookery book I left on the work surface? We need to do some shopping."

"I put it away."

"Well, you'd better get it out again. Have you forgotten that Sue's coming to lunch tomorrow? No answer required. And I nearly tripped over your squash racket in the hall on my way upstairs."

"Had you thought of looking where you were going? OK. OK. I'll move it."

As Kate compiled a list, Hugh looked out of the kitchen window and saw the yellowed leaves of hostas ravaged by slugs and snails. He sighed.

*H*ugh was nominally in charge of the trolley in Waitfare that afternoon. But the trolley had wonky wheels and a mind of its own. If he pushed to the left it went to the right. If he pushed to the right it went to the left. His crabwise progress down the aisles was laborious and slow. He ground to a halt by the biscuits as Kate strode ahead with the list. He glanced half-heartedly at the packets on display. He was bored, not so much with shopping as with life in general.

The job was fine, in its way: Deputy Director of Conservation Policy at the Commission for the Built Heritage and Historic Landscapes in England. The Heritage Commission, for short. The Commission offered advice on the historic environment to anyone who was prepared to listen, and looked after vast tracts of countryside and lots of old buildings for people to go and see. They did, in droves. He liked the work and people seemed to think he did it well. But he had been at the Commission for over ten years, a third of his life. Perhaps it was time he had a change of scene, moved on to pastures new.

And his relationship with Kate? That was fine too, in its way. Quite affectionate, really. More than affectionate. He had no particular complaints, even if she did treat him like a child on occasion. Hadn't she been called 'Bossy Roberts' at school? Things were ticking over well enough but where they were leading he was not sure. How long were he and Kate going to carry on as they were, unmarried and childless in a small house in south London? Hugh had never quite plucked up the courage to broach the subject. Anyway, Kate seemed more focused on building up her homeopathy practice at the moment.

Meanwhile, Hugh pursued his own interests: gardening, books, more books...pictures and antiques, too – when he could afford them. Kate viewed his habits with amused tolerance and gave him a long leash. And there was nothing like some cultivated retail therapy to divert the mind and provide short-term relief. But he needed something more, something to get his teeth into, something to provide a challenge.

He grabbed two packets of fig rolls and resumed his crooked course.

After lunch the next day Hugh gathered up the plates and forks while Kate filled the kettle.

"I liked your lemon tart," said Sue.

"Tarte au citron, if you don't mind, Ms Beckett," said Hugh. "Waitfare's finest. It was a job to remove all the packaging without breaking it in half."

Kate had met Sue a couple of years before when they had joined the local gym on the same day. They were the same age. Where Kate was relaxed about her next birthday Sue viewed the prospect of being thirty and unattached with despair and mounting desperation. She envied Kate her apparently settled relationship with Hugh, even if Kate did complain about him from time to time on the treadmill and the exercise mat. Nothing serious. Just something about the rising tide of books and living in the past half the time.

"What's that whining noise?" said Sue.

"That pleasing and mellifluous sound," said Hugh,

"is Ken, our neighbourhood flautist and plumber, serenading his koi carp. You can just see him through the gap in the fence, sitting on a chair by the pond."

Sue made out a thickset man holding a flute in his large hands with surprising delicacy. "Bit chilly for sitting outside. Is this a habit of his?"

"Ken's been doing it all the time we've known him, which is since we moved here three years ago. Rather nice on a summer evening with a glass of something."

"How come I've not heard it before?"

"He only does it when his wife's out."

"Let's move next door and have our coffee in there," said Hugh. "I'll put on some Miles Davis."

"What's this about your new neighbour?" asked Sue, curling up on the settee. "Is he young and tall with a nice bum?"

"I can't vouch for the last," said Hugh, "but I'd say middle-aged and middle-sized was nearer the mark. He's moved to London from Eastbourne after taking early retirement. Got a big bed, though."

"Thank you, Hugh," said Kate, bringing the mugs into the sitting room.

"I don't seem to have much luck," said Sue. "Why are the nice men always boring? Present company excepted, of course. I saw a poster for Latin American dancing classes on the door of the health food shop. I suppose I might meet someone there."

"A handsome hidalgo with raven hair and a faint

suggestion of garlic. Or a rugged gaucho intent on entwining you with his bolas."

"Ooh, yes!" said Sue, lowering her mug.

"Not on the desk," said Kate. "Hugh won't like it."

"Actually, it's a davenport," said Hugh. "Walnut. It was my mother's."

"Half the drawers won't open," said Kate.

"They're dummy drawers. They're not supposed to."

"Very practical, I must say."

"You'd rather have something in MDF called Malmo or Snorkfart bought in a flatpack."

"At least I could put it together, which is more than I can say for some people."

"Yes, well, I'll just put my coffee on the floor," said Sue. "What's this book on the des...davenport?"

"Another of Hugh's purchases. The wrong half of *The Portrait of a Lady*. Seems to have found its way down from Merseyside. Aren't you from round there?"

"A bit further east," said Sue, opening the book. "Oldham."

"Home of the tubular bandage," said Hugh. "William Cobbett was its MP."

"A little before my time. Oh, St Helen's," said Sue, looking at the inscription on the flyleaf. "I had a friend who used to live there. Wrote to me from time to time. She didn't spell it with an apostrophe, though. Margaret, her name was. She became a vet and got bitten by a snake. The last I heard she'd moved to Formby with a man in soft furnishings. I expect she has millions of kids."

*

"Why are you staring out of the window?" said Kate that evening. "It's pitch dark."

"Just thinking about the book," said Hugh, slowly drawing the curtains. "The Henry James. I wonder who Dorothy Russell was?"

"I don't suppose we'll ever know. What so special about her? It's common enough to find people's names written in second-hand books."

"But not strange notes as well. The occasional post card perhaps, chocolate wrappers used as bookmarks, that sort of thing. This is different."

" 'Fear death by water.' "

"I can't get it out of my mind," said Hugh. "Clever of you to spot it was from *The Waste Land*."

"I was a big fan of Eliot at one time. Sat up with him to all hours in my poky student digs."

"Tom and Kate. Has a certain ring to it."

"Nitwit. Are you going to peel the potatoes or shall I?"

"Do you think it was a warning or threat of some sort?"

"I don't know but I do know we're going to starve at this rate."

"I wonder if Dorothy Russell is still alive."

"Does it matter?" said Kate.

It does to me, thought Hugh. I'm going to find out.

5

*T*elephone, Marjorie," shouted Anthony Buffo from a room upstairs at Toad Books.

The clink of spoon against mug could be heard from the small kitchen behind the panelled green door to the left at the back of the shop. Marjorie emerged with a cup of something steaming and lunged at the instrument on the desk. She picked up the handset but the ringing continued. "Charlie," she said. "You're a bad bird. Making me run like that." She put the cup down on a stained hexagonal mat.

"Who was it?" asked a disembodied voice.

"Only Charlie up to his tricks," said Marjorie, sitting down on her swivel chair and catching her breath. "That boy was in again, wanting to sell some books. He says some of them are old."

"Depends what they are. I'll look at them without commitment. But tell him no book club or ex-library."

*

" 'Pa pa pa pa pa Pa – pa – ge – na.' "

"Charlie's in fine voice this morning," said Hugh, clutching a plastic bottle of milk and some custard creams from the Mini-market next door. "I hope he doesn't know Papageno is a bird catcher."

"I don't think so," said Anthony. "We listened to a tape of *The Magic Flute* on the way to the book fair last Sunday. We had a pretty good day. Came back with a couple of empty boxes. What can I do you for?"

"That book I bought last week. The Henry James you said you got at the auction. I wondered if you could shed any more light on it."

"What sort of light? It's nothing special."

"Like where it came from. Originally."

"As I said before, it was in a box with a whole load of other stuff. I found the box under a pile of corrugated paper while I was having a clear-out upstairs the week before last. I must have bought them ages ago."

"What about the other books in the box?"

"Mostly theatre books and some film annuals."

"Do you still have them?"

"They're over there on the floor by Cinema, TV, Radio and Theatre. Have a look."

Hugh knelt down and set to. He worked his way through several books on the Old Vic and Sadlers Wells, miscellaneous works of theatre criticism, and biographies of actors well known and less well known. Every one had on the flyleaf the name Dorothy Johnson, neatly written in pencil in the top right-hand corner.

"Quite a haul," said Hugh. "The name is different

but the writing is exactly the same. Dorothy Russell must have got married at some stage and changed her name to Johnson."

"Who is Dorothy Russell?"

"The name inside *The Portrait of a Lady*. Dated 1944."

"In that case, someone probably got rid of these when she kicked the bucket. If she was that interested in theatre, and was still in the land of the living, she'd have hung on to them."

"How long ago did you pick them up?"

"I'm not sure. Why do you want to know?"

"It could help me find out who sold the books at the auction."

"Half a mo. I may still have the invoice from Gavel and Gavel. It was in the box with the books." Anthony ran upstairs two steps at a time. Charlie demolished a grape. Marjorie muttered something about the Queen of the Night.

"You're in luck," said Anthony, breathlessly, a few minutes later. "It was in the bin. I got the books three years ago. They were dirt cheap. Rather a crime really. You could always give Gavels a ring to see if they know anything. Try Derek Fox. He's been their books man for years. Take the invoice. Let me know how you get on." Anthony walked slowly back upstairs.

"Anthony's uncharacteristically cheerful," said Hugh.

"Can't think why," said Marjorie. "I don't know how he makes ends meet. And there are those trips to America. This place is practically deserted during the week. All very well for His Lordship. He's out and about picking up even more books while I'm stuck here with only Charlie to talk to."

"He does book fairs and issues the occasional catalogue."

"And advertises in those magazines. Guess who has to take the parcels to the post office and get them all weighed. Even so."

"As you say, even so. Perhaps he has private means."

On his way back to number 40 Dogberry Road Hugh passed number 36, home of the artist Lucy Potter. Whenever he or Kate saw her, she said she was about to move to the wilds of Scotland to find herself and free her spirit – but she never actually did. The gentle crunch of gravel signalled the presence of the artist herself, on her way back from the wheelie bin to her dusky pink front door. Her short black hair was enlivened by an unexpected streak of magenta. Lucy greeted Hugh warmly and invited him in to look at her work in progress. He had bought a picture at her Christmas exhibition the previous year.

He followed Lucy up to her studio on the first floor. The corrugated paper taped to the floor, smooth side up, gave it a strangely spongy feel. A small collection of jam jars held an array of brushes, some bolt upright, others leaning lazily away from the perpendicular. Tubes and sticks of oil and acrylic paints were laid neatly in ice cream tubs. Knives, scissors, and other sharp implements occupied a series of cane baskets on a table at right angles to the front wall. The table formed an L with another table by one of the windows. This was empty but for a pile of sketch books, an anglepoise lamp and a roll of kitchen towels. A vase of rust-coloured chrysanthemums sat on the top of a large plan chest.

"How are things going?" asked Hugh

"A bit up and down. I've got a commission from Quarrendens to do some paintings for their offices in the City. Otherwise, teaching my ladies is keeping the wolf from the door."

"Your picture has been much admired. Why don't you do some more like that?"

"I've moved on. People get used to a certain style but I can't keep doing the same old thing. I need to change, develop. Otherwise, I feel I'm stuck in a rut. I'm working on a series of small pictures loosely based on my sketches of street scenes in Turkey. The first few are on the wall behind you."

Hugh turned. "What lovely colours and shapes," he said. "Curious sense of suspense…menace, almost…in that one, as if something awful were about to happen. They should do well. I do hope so."

"I don't know," said Lucy forlornly. "It's all so unpredictable. I'm beginning to get fed up with London. Perhaps I really will move to Scotland this time."

"Don't do that. We'd miss you."

Kate was lying on the settee when Hugh got home. He said, "I'm a bit worried about Lucy. This hand-to-mouth existence is getting her down. I wish there was something we could do." Kate did not reply. She was fast asleep.

6

*H*ugh was looking at Gavels' website on the computer in the spare room. Kate was peering over his shoulder. An auction, he discovered, was in prospect for Tuesday and Wednesday of the following week. Viewing was on those days and the previous two.

"Furniture and rugs," said Hugh. "Ceramics and glass; toys; pictures and prints; jewellery, silver and plate. No mention of books."

"According to the calendar they're in next month's sale. Still, you could always go and case the joint. The Sunday viewing is on for another couple of hours so you could go today if you put your skates on."

"Why don't you come too?"

"Can't. Sorry. I'm going to the gym with Sue."

Gavels occupied an imposing Edwardian fire station some ten minutes away from Dogberry Road. Cars and vans were scattered randomly on the forecourt, inhibiting access by all but cyclists and those on foot. Hugh parked round the corner and walked back to the building, kicking conkers along the pavement as he went. He stopped to admire the red brick facade, its rectangular windows alternating with pilasters topped by ionic capitals. The ground floor was stone, punctuated on each side by two round windows. The large folding double doors had been retained but entry was through a small and undistinguished door to the right. As Hugh went in he noticed a plaque on the wall: 'This station was opened on the 3rd Day of June 1908 by Arthur Sparks Esq, Chairman of the Fire Brigade Committee of the London County Council.' There was no corresponding commemoration of its closure some ninety years later.

"Catalogue?" barked the girl at reception.

"Er, yes please," said Hugh weakly.

"Three pounds. Furniture and rugs on the ground floor. Everything else upstairs."

Hugh wandered through the assembled rows of tables, chairs and chests of drawers, consulting his catalogue from time to time. He was much taken with a mahogany long case clock and a corner cupboard in the same wood. Two small children were making faces in a tall mirror while their father crawled underneath a Victorian desk, examining its underside with the aid of a torch.

"So that's what a credenza is," shrieked a blousy woman with large jowls and a small husband. "I've always wanted to see one. Look at it, Cyril."

Several people turned to stare at the heavily decorated side cabinet and at the woman's puce companion. Hugh abandoned his inspection of a rosewood library table – William IV, the catalogue informed him – and retreated up the stone steps, narrowly avoiding collision with a stuffed brown bear. It was wearing spectacles and a top hat.

In ceramics and glass Hugh saw a man in a bright red jumper kneeling on the floor with his closely cropped head in a cardboard box. Lot 37: Susie Cooper dinner service. He recognised Peter Gubbins of Peter's Antiques next door to Toad Books.

"I know you, young man," said Peter. "I saw you rummaging chez Buffo the other day. You haven't been into my parlour for a while."

"I bought a jug from you a couple of weeks ago."

"Sorry. You're not after the Clarice Cliff, are you?"

"I was just looking. It's my first visit to Gavels."

"Shame about that vase," said Peter, pointing to the tall cabinet with glass back and sides. "The one on the top shelf. It should be a pair. Not that the catalogue says so, of course. Seems rather lonely on its own, unbalanced somehow. Still, you wouldn't know, if you didn't know, if you see what I mean. And a matching pair would be at least three times the price. Have fun."

Hugh ambled over to the pictures. Some were hung on the walls, others stacked vertically on shelves, others piled on a table with a pale blue formica top. Several people were leafing through the portfolios in the browsers at either end of the table. A large portrait of a man in Regency dress was displayed on an easel.

"What's the difference between 'attributed to', 'circle of', 'follower of', and 'manner of'?" Hugh asked an effete young man with floppy brown hair much the colour of his own.

"The terms are explained in the front of the catalogue."

"So they are. I'm rather a novice when it comes to auctions."

"Are you interested in a particular painting?"

"What can you tell me about this one?" Hugh took from the shelf a small watercolour of a church in a wooded landscape. A few figures were in the foreground. One appeared to have a dog.

"English School. Early nineteenth century. Might be Archibald Kettle but then again it might not."

"So you wouldn't attribute it to him, then?"

"No. A respectable provenance, though," said the effete young man, pointing to the label on the back. It bore the name of a gallery in South Kensington. "Closed some years ago but it had a good reputation in its day."

"How do people bid if they can't be here? You seem to hold auctions when most people are at work."

"You can leave a commission bid with the receptionist. The auctioneer then bids on your behalf. There's a form in the back of the catalogue and spares up at the front."

"How do I know what to bid?"

"There are estimates against each lot in the catalogue. But things can go for a lot less or a lot more, depending on the interest on the day. So it's pot luck, I'm afraid."

"Thank you," said Hugh. "I'll think about it."

On the way out, he braved the receptionist. "Do you happen to know if Derek Fox is around? I wanted a word with him about some books."

"Derek doesn't come in on Sundays if there are no books in the viewing. He should be here tomorrow. Or you could give him a ring. The number's in the catalogue." She disappeared into an office with a large round window.

Returning to his Peugeot, Hugh contemplated the attractions of flexible working. If he worked at home on Tuesday he could go to the auction himself. He found the prospect rather exciting, if a little daunting. As he fumbled in his pocket for the keys he noticed that the battered estate car on the other side of the road was just like Anthony Buffo's.

7

*T*he prevailing fashion for open plan offices had not yet infected the Commission for the Built Heritage and Historic Landscapes in England. The accommodation in a 1930s block somewhere in the West End was cramped but afforded privacy. This suited Hugh as he prepared to telephone Derek Fox from his office on the fourth floor. He saw that the number in the catalogue differed from the one on the invoice Anthony had given him in almost every respect. He tried the one in the catalogue.

"Good morning. Gavel and Gavel. Lorna speaking. How may I help you?"

"I'd like to speak to Derek Fox, please."

"Who shall I say is calling?"

"My name is Mullion. Hugh Mullion."

"One moment, please." Hugh doodled as he waited.

"Derek Fox here," came a languid voice. "Would you like us to try and sell some books for you?"

"Actually, it's about some you've already sold. One in particular. I got it the other day from Anthony Buffo at Toad Books. I gather he bought it in a lot from Gavels about three years ago. I was trying to trace the seller. Anthony suggested that I had a word with you."

"Did he indeed? That's rather naughty of Tony. He ought to know that we act strictly as intermediaries between vendors and purchasers and maintain the confidentiality of both. We would never reveal a vendor's identity to a purchaser or to anyone else."

"Couldn't you get in touch with the seller and ask them to contact me, if they didn't mind?" said Hugh. "I could give you my address and phone number."

"I'm afraid not. It's not a service we provide, even if we still had the vendor's details. We had a new computer system at the beginning of last year and lost a whole load of stuff. Sorry but there we are. Give my regards to Tony."

Hugh walked back from the station that evening, feeling frustrated and strangely unsettled. So much for trying to do something, to find out more about the blue book and the note inside it. He had got nowhere. Now what? Bin Ends' offer of Brouilly provided a brief distraction. Bottles clinking, Hugh paused when he came to Peter's Antiques. A notice on the door declared the shop closed. A couple of table lamps illuminated the pale lemon interior, the bulbs reflected in the glass of a large picture of a steam frigate hanging from the wall. A notice on the door of Toad Books next door also claimed that the shop was closed but the door itself was wide open. All the lights in the shop were on. Charlie, firmly in his cage, was occupied in the destruction of some apple wood twigs. Anthony was transferring piles of books from one part of the shop to another, a pencil lodged behind his right ear. The table that usually stood outside was folded near Charlie's cage. The familiar satsuma boxes of allegedly bargain books were lying on the floor.

"I'm trying to sort things out before they get hopelessly out of control," said Anthony as Hugh hovered on the threshold. "All the books on the stairs need pricing, the books on the floor need to be on the shelves, and the books on the shelves need culling to make the space."

"What will happen to those?"

"They'll join the ranks of bargain books and be put outside. I think it's time Ethel M Dell and Rafael Sabatini were given an airing. No one seems to read them anymore. I'm in two minds about Jeffery Farnol."

"You've got hours of work on your hands. You surely can't do it all tonight."

"No, but I'd like to make some progress."

"I'll leave you in peace then."

"I didn't mean that," said Anthony. "Any luck with Derek Fox?"

"Sadly not. He said divulging the name of the seller would breach confidentiality and they might not have the records any more in any case. So I'm no further forward. He sends you his regards, by the way."

"I do think he could have been a bit more helpful. Leave it with me. I've known Derek a long time."

"Thank you. Was that your car I saw near Gavels yesterday?"

"Could well have been. I popped in briefly to see what they had."

As Hugh was about to go, he noticed that the panelled green doors to the right at the back of the bookshop were open a little way. By the light from the main part of the shop he could just make out more boxes and rolls of bubblewrap.

"What exactly do you keep in those rooms?"

"Exactly what's in them I can't say. Generally speaking, it's more books, wrapping materials and things I haven't got space for elsewhere."

"Sounds like our spare bedroom."

"I hope that's less chaotic. I must get round to clearing them out and putting them to better use."

As Hugh was leaving he passed Spiro from the Minimarket with a bag of lychees for Charlie.

---

8

*H*ugh had had little difficulty in persuading his boss Roger, the Director of Conservation Policy, that he would be better working on his presentation at home. 'Prevention is better than cure: a proactive approach to conserving the historic environment' was the theme, a selection of worthies from the heritage world the intended audience. Hugh hoped that Kate could show him how to do PowerPoint slides when she came home that evening. He normally relied on his secretary, Belinda, to do those for him. He set to work on the text of his presentation but his mind was on the auction, the first he had been to in all his years of accumulating. He was feeling increasingly apprehensive. The catalogue said that pictures and prints were due to start at 1.30p.m. Hugh thought he had better get there early just in case.

"Are you bidding?" the receptionist asked Hugh as he walked through the door clutching his catalogue. She looked a good deal more friendly than the girl who had barked at him at the viewing.

"I hope to be," he said.

"You'll need a paddle number, then," she said, cheerfully. "Fill in this registration form and I'll give you a number. You give the number to the auctioneer if you make a successful bid. That way we know the identity of the purchaser but everyone else doesn't. Except, of course, that most people know each other anyway. It tends to be the same crowd of dealers every time." In exchange for the form Hugh received a piece of stiff white card bearing three bold black numbers: 734. It was a little larger than a postcard. He went upstairs, as directed.

There was a short break between the completion of ceramics and glass and the start of pictures and prints. A porter was removing chairs from a stack and putting them out at the front to supplement those already there. Hugh worked his way to the back and found an empty chair. The old hands were swapping stories about the remarkable bargains they had picked up only the week before in Kent or Sussex, and the remarkable prices they had already obtained for them.

The auctioneer mounted the rostrum and called the proceedings to order. He was none other than the effete young man from two days before, now invested with an unexpected gravitas and authority. The room went quiet. Hugh gulped. He saw Peter Gubbins leaving with two bulging carrier bags.

"Good afternoon, ladies and gentlemen. Sorry about

the delay. Slight technical hitch with the computer. Before we get going, may I please ask you to switch off any mobile phones and pagers? The first lot – lot 860 over there – is *Still life with a green bowl and walnuts*, together with two other pictures. Who will start me at £80?"

Hugh was taken aback by the speed with which the lots came and went. Porters held aloft the pictures they could reach and pointed to those they could not. As he had been told, many were sold for much less than the estimates, a few for much more. Some attracted no bids at all. Occasionally an estimate proved to be spot on. As the lot numbers went higher Hugh began to feel an unpleasant gnawing in the pit of his stomach. He wanted to be sick.

"We come now to lot 903: *Church in a wooded landscape.*" Hugh squirmed. "Quite a bit of interest in this one." Hugh panicked. "I have a couple of commission bids. Let's start on £100. 110 at the front. 120 in the aisle. 130 at the front. 140 in the aisle." Hugh was paralysed with fear. But he wanted the picture. "Any advance on £140? Are we all done at £140?" Hugh forced up a hand roughly to the level of his right ear. "150 at the back. A new bidder." Heads turned. "160 in the aisle. 170 at the back. 180 in the aisle. 190 at the back." The fair-haired woman in black standing in the aisle shook her head curtly at the auctioneer. "Are we all done at £190? Thank you. 734."

Hugh lowered his card and went to get a cup of tea and a flapjack in the small side-room that passed for a café. He was exhausted and his shirt was sticking to his back. The nervousness had passed. He felt light-headed and curiously elated. Not just because he had got the picture he wanted. Once he had started bidding he had enjoyed the competition itself – and beating the woman in black.

On his way home with the picture loosely wrapped in thick grey paper on the back seat of the car, Hugh wondered what he would tell Kate, a prospect more frightening than the auction itself. Not only had he bid more than he had intended but he had quite forgotten the buyer's premium: fifteen per cent plus VAT. No more Brouilly for a while, then; strictly plonk.

9

*H*is presentation complete, Hugh went downstairs that evening to join Sue in the sitting room. Kate was bellowing into a mobile phone in the kitchen.

"Kate says you're trying to find out more about that book you bought."

"The Henry James, yes. I don't seem to be getting very far."

"You could probably find the other volume on the internet."

"Probably. But it wouldn't be the same; it wouldn't be the right copy. Anyway, it's not so much the book of the story I'm interested in as the story of the book. That, and the owner."

"The mysterious Dorothy?"

"Yes. But it's over sixty years ago since Dorothy Russell wrote her name in it. Not much prospect of finding her after all that time. She's probably dead by now."

"If you find her you might find the other volume too."

"Not very likely. Why chuck out one volume and keep the other?"

"I suppose you're right. Pity, though. You could have killed two birds with one stone."

"How?"

"I mean you could have completed the portraits of two ladies. Dorothy and...whoever it was Henry James wrote about. I've never read the book."

"Neither have I," said Hugh, twisting round to select a CD from the rack.

"Hugh. Turn that noise down. I'm trying to talk to my mother. The line's awful as it is."

"Ms Roberts is referring to 'So What?'," said Hugh, pressing the button a couple of times. "One of Miles' best in my humble estimation. Kate prefers Elgar. Stirring stuff but a bit sentimental. How was your gaucho? Did you reel from the stench of horse sweat as he grabbed you for a tango?"

"No such luck. I got stuck with a boring bloke in coffee futures with acne and red braces."

"I expect he has a Porsche and goes hang-gliding at weekends."

"I doubt it," said Sue glumly. "I'll give it another week. Then perhaps I'll enter a nunnery."

"What are we going to do with you?" asked Hugh softly.

"Dunno," said Sue, cradling a glass of Bin Ends'

cheapest red in her small white hands. Hugh noticed that her nails were the same colour as the wine. "Any eligible men at the Commission?"

"The ones I know are already spoken for or else have beards."

Kate marched in from the kitchen and slammed the door. "What's that about beards? Oh, never mind. Honestly, my mother."

"Do I detect a degree of exasperation?"

"Too right. She kept going on about hair and children."

"What about children's hair?"

"My hair and our children."

"We don't have any," said Hugh.

"That's the point. Isn't it about time we started, she said? I'm not getting any younger, she said. She's always wanted grandchildren, she said."

"And what did you say?"

"I told her that I didn't want to be lumbered with bloody kids just at the moment, thank you very much, and there was plenty of time anyway."

"I see."

"And then she asked what you thought."

"What did you say?"

"I told her you weren't in a hurry."

"I see."

"Said you weren't ready to settle down."

"I see."

"Will you stop saying 'I see'."

"Maybe we should discuss it sometime."

"So what about the hair?" asked Sue, seeing advantage in interruption.

"She said it made me look like a tart."

"Charming," said Hugh. "Is your mother well versed in the ways of tarts?"

"When did she see it?" asked Sue.

"A couple of weeks or so ago. Just after it was done. At least she didn't go on about kids then."

"I haven't met your mum," said Sue.

"Count yourself fortunate," said Kate. "She means well but she drives me round the bend."

"What about your mum, Hugh?" asked Sue.

"She's dead," he said. He paused for a moment. "She died a couple of years ago. Hence the davenport. She knew I liked it so she left it to me. My father lives in splendid isolation in deepest Sussex. We see him from time to time."

"Sounds lonely," said Sue.

"He potters about and tends his garden. Kipling keeps him company."

"Kipling?"

"His cat. A large ginger beast with a fondness for cornflakes and blancmange."

"I'd better be going," said Sue. "Night, Kate. See you. Don't worry about the hair. It suits you."

"Thanks."

"I'll see you out," said Hugh.

By the open front door Sue looked up at Hugh and said, "Look after yourself, won't you. And look after Kate too."

"She's feeling a bit pressured, what with one thing and another."

"She's luckier than she realises. Some of us haven't got past first base. I like the picture, by the way." Sue was looking at *Church in a wooded landscape* already hanging on the hall wall.

"Thank you. Kate seems not wholly averse to it either. I was expecting forty lashes at least."

"I'd better stop letting the cold air in. Night, Hugh." She kissed him gently on the cheek.

10

Orange pansies had replaced the geraniums in the pot outside the door of Toad Books. Variegated ivy trailed down the side. A collection of works of natural history had supplanted the long-standing display of items of local history in the window. A monograph on the mole was prominent amongst the new arrivals. Looking through the window, Hugh saw Charlie on the top of his cage, making short work of the yolk of a hard-boiled egg. He went inside. Marjorie was conspicuous by her absence. A furtive man in rustling waterproofs was in close communion with some books in the corner ostensibly about health.

Hugh nodded to Anthony, who was standing by the open doors of the cabinet behind the desk. He was talking to a short man wearing a checked cap.

"I don't call this a 'good copy'," said the man, tapping the book he held in his left hand. "Your catalogue says it's good. It's not good at all. I don't want it now."

"In booksellers' parlance 'good' means 'not very good'. The standard terms and definitions are set out in the front of the catalogue. As it happens, a much better copy has come in," said Anthony, removing a book in almost mint condition from the cabinet. "This is a fine copy in a fine dust wrapper. More expensive, of course, but I might be able to do something on it if you're interested."

"Now that's more like it."

Hugh loitered by the remainder table in the middle of the shop. The table was piled with multiple copies of the same books. They were brand new but much reduced in price. Hugh was looking at the pictures in the middle of a thick biography of a Victorian Prime Minister when Anthony joined him.

"I had lunch with Derek Fox the other day and encouraged him to be a bit more co-operative," said Anthony. "He's trawled through Gavels' records and found the name of the person who sold those books. And two other lots too, it turns out. He still wouldn't tell me the name at first but I got him to ring the seller and ask if he would mind your getting in touch with him."

"He?"

"Yes. One Colin Smedley."

"Not Johnson?" said Hugh. He sounded downcast.

"No. He lives in Kent, apparently. This is his number," said Anthony, producing a small piece of paper from the top pocket of his shirt. "I'm not sure how much he knows but you can try him anyway. Evenings and weekends."

"Well done. Thank you." Hugh put the piece of paper in his wallet.

"That's all right. Derek owes me one."

"Where's Marjorie, by the way?"

"She's been whisked away for a mystery weekend by the elusive Mr T. A significant anniversary for Marjorie. I am sworn to secrecy but it could be between fifty-nine and sixty-one." Hugh and Anthony moved towards Classics to let a man with a thin red beard examine the remaindered gardening books.

"Are we allowed to know what the T stands for?"

"Between you, me and the remainder table it's... Turbot."

Hugh sniggered.

"Marjorie's rather sensitive about it. Seems she's been the butt of endless fish jokes. Believe it or not her maiden name was Brill, like the Katherine Mansfield short story. Don't for heaven's sake let her know I told you."

"I shall be the soul of discretion."

Anthony groaned and pointed to the door.

As he walked back down Dogberry Road Hugh saw Kate talking to their new neighbour, Gordon West, outside number 42. He slowed down and lurked behind a cherry tree, pretending to do up a recalcitrant shoelace. When Kate and Gordon had finished and gone their separate ways, Hugh resumed his course. Shortly afterwards, he put his key in the door of number 40.

After a decent interval, he ambled into the kitchen and said casually:

"Was that Gordon West I saw you talking to?"

"Oh. Yes." Kate was arranging lilies in a vase.

"Settling in, is he?"

"Seems to be."

"I wonder what he does. I thought people went *to* Eastbourne when they retired."

"Early retirement. He said he wanted to start a new life. He separated from his wife not long ago."

"I see."

"And he was interested when I said I was a homeopath. Didn't give me the 'eye of newt and toe of frog' routine. Unlike some people I could mention. He asked me to take his case sometime."

"It's nice you're getting on so well with Mr West."

"Not jealous, are you?" said Kate, taking the flowers into the sitting room.

"Good Lord, no."

11

The following evening Hugh rang the number on the piece of paper Anthony had given him. His excitement at the prospect of progress was tempered by a nagging sense of unease. A child answered after what seemed an inordinate length of time. She brought her father to the phone.

"Hello. My name's Hugh Mullion. Derek Fox from Gavels spoke to you recently about some books you sold at the auction."

"It was a few years back now. We were clearing out my mother's house in Surrey. We kept some of the books ourselves but there were three boxes to get rid of. I thought the simplest thing was to give them to a charity shop but Alison – that's my wife – said we might as well try and get something for them. So I took them to Gavels. Sold them all but I can't say we got much, especially after the commission. Hardly worth it, really."

"I was interested in one box in particular. Mostly theatre books."

"I remember those. I don't think my mother ever looked at them. They were in that box for years. Her next door neighbour insisted on giving them to her when she moved."

"What was her name?"

"Dorothy Johnson. Dorothy and George Johnson. Mad about theatre, they were. Makes you wonder why she turfed out the books. She was rather a local celebrity. Always had her name in the *Advertiser*. She spent a lot of time acting. On stage and off, we used to say. Bit of a *grande dame*, if you know what I mean."

"And George?"

"Pretty normal. Let it all wash over him as far as I could see. They kept costumes in the loft and the garage was full of props. Mind you, it was a great place to play when we were kids. Dorothy caught me wearing a turban once. I expected an explosion but she just laughed and said it suited me."

"Did Dorothy and George have children too?"

"Michael and Jennifer. They were older than me and my sister. I'm thirty-nine, before you ask."

"How long ago did the Johnsons move?"

"Must have been about twenty years ago, when George retired."

"Are they still alive?"

"I'm afraid I've no idea what happened to them or where they went. I think my mother and Dorothy corresponded for a while but then lost touch. Even the

Christmas cards dried up."

"What about Michael and Jennifer? They must be living and working somewhere."

"I expect so but I haven't got a clue where. I think they'd both left home before Dorothy and George moved. Anyway, I must go. Alison's calling me for my supper. Sorry I can't be more help. It's a long time ago now."

That's it then, thought Hugh. At least I tried.

12

"Much excitement at the Commission meeting today," said Hugh, struggling with the corkscrew in the kitchen. "Miss Twitchett choked on her brie and grape sandwich and Professor Arkwright burst into tears."

"What provoked this unseemly display?" asked Kate, standing, arms folded, with her back to the sink.

"Our Chairman revealed to the astonished company that he had been elected Principal of an Oxford college from next January. Apparently, the current Principal is retiring unexpectedly on grounds of ill health. They wanted a successor in quickly."

"So the days of Sir Richard at the Commission are numbered. Rather short notice, isn't it?"

"I can't believe they'll get someone else appointed by the time he goes. Nifty footwork isn't quite the Ministry's thing." Hugh removed the cork with an air of triumph and poured a couple of glasses of wine. "Still, it was a welcome diversion from the main business of the meeting – inclusive definitions of the historic environment. The archaeologists were being even more difficult than usual. The Director of the Wider Awareness Network spent half an hour on the role of memory in defining a sense of place. The developers kept going on about aspic and ossification and Miss Bee slept soundly throughout."

"Miss Bee?"

"The representative of the Landscape Appreciation Society. At least the biscuits completed their *tour de table* this time. The biscuit plate usually gets stuck in front of her and she works her way through the lot. There's nothing worse at a meeting than people who won't pass the biscuits. Miss Bee affects hardness of hearing when the matter is brought to her attention."

"Should be a good farewell party if Sir Richard runs true to form." Kate came forward to claim her glass. "Perhaps he'll give a repeat performance of 'Nina' – from Argentina. Commission Christmas parties won't be the same without him and Noel Coward. Is he going back to his old college?"

"I don't think there were any men at St Helen's in his day. Well, not officially, anyway."

"Did you say St Helen's?"

"I did."

"You don't suppose..?"

"What?"

"Don't be obtuse, Hugh. The inscription in the book. Maybe your Dorothy was at Oxford not on Merseyside during the war."

"You could be right. Remember what Sue said about the apostrophe. But the trail's run cold. She vanished into thin air twenty years ago."

"You could always try the college. Why don't you check their website?"

13

*H*ugh closed the door of his office and rang the number he had found.

"St Helen's College," said the voice at the other end of the telephone. Hugh detected a slight burr.

"I'd like to speak to the College Secretary, Mrs Rainbow, please."

"Mrs Rainbow has just gone on maternity leave. Again. I'll put you through to her assistant, Lydia Featherstonehaugh."

"College Office," said a jolly girl. "Can I help you?"

"I'm trying to check if someone was at St Helen's during the war and if you know anything about them."

"Gosh. That's a long time ago. I think you need the Development Office. They know about Senior Members and things. I would transfer you but I don't know which button to press. I'm afraid you'll have to go through the Lodge again. Byeee."

Hugh repeated his request to Deidre Greene in the Development Office.

"When did Dorothy Russell matriculate?" she asked briskly. "In what year did she come up?"

"I don't know but she seems to have been at St Helen's in 1944 so then or a year or two before, I suppose."

On checking, Miss Greene was able to confirm that Dorothy Russell went up to Oxford in 1943 from a rather smart school in the West of England. Her subject was English. There was no record of marriage and a change of name to Dorothy Johnson.

"Do you happen to have an address for her?" asked Hugh.

"Addresses of our Senior Members are treated as confidential to the College and to the Senior Members' Association. So I couldn't tell you even if we did. However, it looks as though we've never had an address for her. Not since she came up, anyway. Must be one of our longest-standing Missing Members, assuming she's still alive. Helen's women are pretty hardy so I wouldn't rule it out."

"I wonder if she kept in touch with any of her contemporaries?"

"If she did, they haven't passed on an address for her. The College magazine regularly asks for information about those who've sunk without trace."

"Looks like I'm out of luck."

"One thing you could do is try the Senior Members' Association directory on the College website. That gives e-mail addresses for those who've got e-mail and don't mind giving their addresses out for anyone to see. There may be one or two from the 1943 vintage."

"I'll try it. Thank you for your trouble."

"My pleasure. We like a challenge in the Development Office. It makes a change from the new building appeal fund."

14

Gordon sounds cheerful," said Hugh, as the strains of Rodgers and Hart's 'Manhattan' penetrated the party wall. He plumped his slate-grey pillows and prepared to climb into bed beside Kate. "Must be all those girls we keep seeing him with. I wonder how he manages it?"

"It's called charm," said Kate.

"He must be old enough to be their father."

"There's something to be said for experience. He's wearing pretty well too."

"Oh is he?"

"Purely a professional interest. I took his case the other day, remember."

"Any startling revelations?"

"I couldn't tell you, even if there were. You know that."

"Every time I ask anybody anything these days they say it's confidential," said Hugh plaintively. "I'm beginning to think there's a conspiracy."

"No luck with your old biddies then?"

"If you mean St Helen's Senior Members, there were two listed under 1943 in the directory. I've sent them both e-mails. One replied almost immediately saying she didn't remember a Dorothy Russell, and had no information on her whereabouts. I haven't heard from the other."

Kate was setting the alarm for the morning as Gordon turned Manhattan into an isle of joy, again.

"You don't think you're carrying this a bit far?" she said. "I agree the note's intriguing but this is developing into an obsession."

"Why do you keep helping me if you think I'm obsessed?" said Hugh indignantly. "You put me on to the college in the first place."

"I like helping you. But I do think you should bring this Dorothy thing to a conclusion one way or the other soon. It's all you seem to think about these days."

"I don't like to admit defeat," said Hugh, turning off the main light from the switch above the bed. "You know me. Once I've got the bit between my teeth. The trouble is, I'm no further forward than I was at the start."

"You know more than you did about Dorothy."

"I suppose so. And I got that picture because of the Gavels' connection."

"There you are then. Of course, you could always ring the M Johnsons in the London telephone directory, assuming the son lives in London."

"I've already looked. There are loads of M Johnsons

in the book. I can't ring all of them on the off-chance. I'm beginning to go off the idea after all. It obviously isn't meant."

"Thank goodness that's over."
   "I think Gordon has rather a nice voice."
   "Oh really?" said Hugh, moving closer.
   "I just want to get to the end of my chapter."
   "The cover is revolting. It's like pink marshmallow."
   "Haven't you got a good book to read?"
   "I have indeed. *The Lost Rivers of London*. I've done the Walbrook and the Fleet and I'm just setting off down the Tyburn."
   But Hugh was not concentrating on rivers lost, stolen or temporarily mislaid. He was thinking of a different book. He had not really gone off the idea at all, just did not know what to do next. He turned over and sighed.
   Was he obsessed, as Kate had said? Of course not. Merely focussed and persistent. Or so he told himself.

15

The sign on the door of Toad Books said CLOSED. It was. Hugh peered through the door. He peered through the window. The books from outside were inside and the table folded up by Charlie's dustbin. Both cage and parrot were absent. The sign on the door of Peter's Antiques said OPEN. It was – slightly ajar. There were two salmon-pink Lloyd Loom chairs and a box of bits and pieces outside. As Hugh went into the shop a piercing two-tone electronic sound came from the back. The table lamps he had seen previously were both on, as were a standard lamp with a parchment shade and a large oil lamp, converted to electricity. The cosy scene was quite deserted.

"Hello," said Hugh, weaving between a cast iron umbrella stand and a pair of balloon back chairs. "Hello." The pile of plates on the circular tea table wobbled dangerously. The rocking horse rocked. "Hello."

"I'm out the back with Jemima," returned Peter Gubbins.

Hugh stumbled past some old newspapers and a carpet sweeper, and out through the back door.

"Hello, you. Hasn't she got wonderful curves?" said Peter, swelling with pride. "I thought I'd give her a quick polish in a spare moment." The dark green paintwork of the car parked in the service road behind the shop shone in the autumn sun.

"What do you think of her aerodynamic styling?"

"Very smart," said Hugh. "What is it?"

"*She*," said Peter, a trifle peevishly, "is a Jowett Javelin. They were only made between 1947 and 1953. Not as reliable as they might have been. Let down by the engine and gear box. But I've no complaints about Jemima. She handles beautifully. Lots of room inside too."

"She's in lovely condition," said Hugh, redeeming himself. "I hope I look as good when I'm that age." Music to Peter's ears. "I was wondering if you knew where Anthony was. The place is like the *Marie Celeste*."

"The *bouquiniste* has crossed the pond. Dashed off to New York again. Muggins here is looking after Charlie. Usually Anthony's friend does it when he's away but he couldn't this time."

"So where *is* Charlie?"

"Back at my place. Make sure you tell Charlie where you're going if you go out, he said, and say goodnight to him when you go to bed. That bird is quite convinced he's human. Said something about a champagne cork yesterday evening. Gave me quite a turn. Anthony brought him round a couple of nights ago and shot off backwards shouting, 'Don't forget to feed the parrot.' "

"When will he be back?"

"He said he'd be a few days, whatever that means."

"What does Anthony do in New York? He was there a few weeks ago."

"He just said on business. I don't know what, though."

"All very rum and mysterious," said Hugh, watching a black and white cat slinking into one of the garages opposite. "And no Marjorie either."

"No. I think she did something to her back when she was away last weekend."

"The mind boggles. She reminds me of one of those Beryl Cook women, watching male strippers and holding a glass of stout."

"She's a dark horse, that one," said Peter.

"As is Anthony Buffo. I'll leave you to your waxing and polishing."

He made his way down the service road towards the high street in search of a crusty cob.

16

*H*ugh lumbered through the kitchen, clutching his filthy load as if his life depended on it. He was bent at an angle of forty-five degrees.

"It's freezing with both the doors open," said Kate. "And you're dropping bits on the floor."

"I'm being as quick as I can," he said. "They're even heavier than your homeopathy books." He deposited his cargo carefully on the York stone paving at the back.

"What are you going to do with them?"

"Edge those beds. They're the original Victorian rope-top tiles. They cost a fortune now. Lucky I saw them in that skip."

"You made enough noise getting them out. I wouldn't mind a pond with a small stream or a fountain. The sound of running water is relaxing."

"A water feature isn't compulsory. You'll be wanting koi carp next so you can play soothing music to them, like Ken."

"I haven't played my guitar for ages. You could put a pond there," said Kate, pointing through the window.

"Certainly not," said Hugh crossly. "That's the bed with the crab apple my father gave us. I've just planted those wallflowers round it. Orange Bedder, they're called. Makes a change from all that yellow in spring."

"Right. That's the lot," said Hugh, closing the kitchen door with his foot. "Any chance of some coffee?"

"There might be. Even for a horticultural imperialist."

"I just like things to be right. Think of the injuries I sustain." Hugh presented his grazed hands for inspection.

"I've no sympathy," said Kate. "I've told you to wear gloves. Wash your hands and have one of those," she said, removing from the dresser a small brown bottle with a white plastic lid. "Ledum. I ought to buy it in bulk."

"Thank you, Miss Nightingale. I gather Lucy did all right at the Battersea art fair. Sold quite a few pictures and got a lot of names and addresses in that book she put out. Augurs well for her Christmas open weekend."

"Let's hope so. By the way, a man rang while you were on one of your journeys to and from the skip. It was Colin Smedley. The one you spoke to before about the Dorothy books. I wrote his number on the top of the supplement on the Bolivian economy. There."

"What did he want?"

"I don't know. He just asked if you would ring him."

*

With clean and smarting hands, Hugh went into the sitting room and pressed the requisite buttons.

"Thanks for ringing back. I mentioned our conversation to my wife, Alison. She suggested I look in my mother's old address book. I kept it for sentimental reasons. We turned the place upside down and couldn't find it. Then our Rebecca found it in the video when she tried to put a tape in. Young William must have put in there. It was the devil of a job to get it out."

"Anything of interest in the address book?"

"An address and telephone number for Dorothy Johnson. Somewhere in Dorset."

Part Two

17

Hugh's initial euphoria at having Dorothy Johnson's address gave way to doubt and uncertainty. Now what? Twenty years was a long time. She could be dead or in a home or living with one of her children by now. If she had gone up to Oxford in 1943 she must be about eighty. It sounded as though George was even older. Always assuming he was still around, of course. Even if Dorothy was at the house in Dorset, Hugh had no idea what he should do. He could hardly ring her out of the blue and say he had found the second volume of a book she had acquired over sixty years earlier. Nor could he reasonably quiz her about a note consisting of no more than an initial and four words. And he had no real proof that Dorothy Johnson and Dorothy Russell were one and the same, though the coincidence of identical handwriting and first names was pretty compelling. Hugh agonised.

*

"Hugh," said Kate. "Stop agonising. You're wandering around like a lost soul. Just decide what you want to do and do it."

"Well, I would if I knew what to do. And this weather doesn't help. It's depressing."

"Clocks go back tonight."

"So it'll get dark even earlier. That's even more depressing."

"For heaven's sake. Have a cup of tea and a Kit-Kat."

"You just want to soften me up to look at your brochure. Difficult to think about water features when it's raining."

"Look," said Kate. "These ones are wall fountains. No plumbing required and specially guaranteed to preserve crab apples and wallflowers. Then there are these other ones. Round bowl; square bowl; single; double; with pebbles and amphora or without."

"Hm. I suppose I could look her up in the telephone directory. At least see if she's still there. We've got a complete set at work. In the library – or 'learning resource centre', as we have to call it now."

"Honestly. It's like talking to a brick wall."

18

Dorothy came in from the garden and read the letter again. It was a short letter and she had already read it several times. She went into the kitchen where George was washing his hands at the sink.

"We need to decide what I should I do about this," said Dorothy, sitting down at the table. She was looking rather pale.

"Tricky, isn't it? He's taken a lot of trouble to find you. He must be pretty enterprising."

"Yes. But why do it at all?"

"The letter's not very clear about that. How was he to know you hadn't got rid of it deliberately? If you had, you'd hardly want it back, would you?"

"I'd forgotten all about the book."

"We've still got Volume I. It's with the other Henry James in the study. I suppose it would be nice to have Volume II back for the sake of completeness, though we seem to have survived without it for the last twenty

71

years." George dried his hands and joined Dorothy at the table.

"I don't know how it got into that box of books I gave to Hermione Smedley. I didn't even know she'd died. Three years ago, apparently."

"You didn't keep in touch."

"I feel rather guilty about that now. She must have been a good ten years younger than me. Makes you think."

"You could ask him to send it."

"Doesn't seem quite adequate in the circumstances. I wonder what he's like?"

19

*H*ugh recognised the writing on the pale blue envelope immediately. Perhaps a little shakier than it once was but unmistakable all the same. He tore open the envelope and read the letter as he went back down the hall, narrowly avoiding the purple and yellow vacuum cleaner standing by the cupboard under the stairs.

Kate was sitting at the kitchen table flicking through her copy of *Aphrodite*, a small magazine to which she and several of her friends had switched after many years' loyal readership of a larger and more expensive one. "What does she say?" asked Kate, without looking up.

"You can read the letter, if you like," said Hugh. "Basically, she confirms that she was Dorothy Russell before she got married in the 1950s, George is alive and kicking, she thinks I'm jolly clever to have tracked her down, and why don't we come and visit her sometime?"

"We?" Kate looked up. "Did you mention me in your letter to her?"

"No. She just says I'd be welcome to bring my partner."

"Rather an enlightened term for one so old."

"Perhaps you misjudge her. Are you coming?"

"Why? Are you going?"

"I rather thought I might. Seems churlish to refuse when I wrote to her in the first place and worse to say yes and do nothing about it. And I'd like to take the book with me. She says she remembers it."

"You could post it."

"That's not really the point. She's not just a name in blue-black ink on the flyleaf any more. She's a real person, apparently *compos mentis*, and I'd like to meet her. I might discover something about the note too."

"All sounds rather embarrassing to me. Also, it's Dorset. Not like a quick visit to your father in Sussex. Or to my parents in Essex, come to that."

"It's not that far, though perhaps a bit much to go there and back in a day."

"You're not suggesting we stay with her as well?"

"No. We could go down and spend the night in a hotel or bed and breakfast and go and see Dorothy and George the next day. She said Sunday lunch."

"Isn't this getting rather expensive?"

"We could find somewhere cheap on the internet."

"Oh could we?" said Kate.

"And we'd need to set off at a respectable hour on

the Saturday to make it worth our while. I don't want
to arrive in the dark anyway."

"This would be a Saturday when I'm not at the
Centre, would it?"

"Ah."

"Or going to my class at the gym?"

"I'm sure missing one wouldn't do any harm. Nothing
wrong with your legs, tum or bum."

"Flattery will get you nowhere."

"You should be pleased I want you to come."

"You just want me to navigate. I assume it would
be car not train."

"There hasn't been a station round there for forty
years, thanks to Dr Beeching."

"Look," said Kate gently. "This is something you need
to do on your own. I'd just be in the way. But I'll help
with the route, if you like."

20

*H*ugh stopped at a service station somewhere north of Winchester at a time when he might otherwise have been rummaging in the boxes outside Toad Books. A sullen youth with acne and stiff gelled hair directed him to a table in the non-smoking section. Smoke drifted into it from a table on the other side of the low trellis divide. Hugh poured himself some coffee from the pot and brushed the crumbs of his Maryland cookie from the map in front of him. He was feeling apprehensive. What would Dorothy be like? A bit of a *grande dame*, Colin Smedley had said. Or George, for that matter? Sounded fairly resilient, but that was twenty years ago. What on earth would he talk about for all that time? Perhaps George would come to the rescue, but he must be well over eighty. It was too late to back out now. Hugh would have liked Kate's moral support.

He studied her instructions, neatly written in a firm, sensible hand on a small piece of squared paper, and tried to follow the prescribed route from London to Okeminster on the map. He was distracted from his half-hearted efforts at reconciliation by sight of the spectacular array of sauces and other condiments in colour-coded sachets on the counter nearby. He appraised the colour chosen for each, carefully considering how far it reflected the contents of the sachet concerned. Before he could form a definitive judgement about purple for vinegar and blue for tartare sauce, a piercing scream from a small child, reprimanded for unwinding the artificial ivy from the trellis, brought him back to full consciousness. Time I was on my way, he thought. Another couple of hours should do it.

The sun on the beeches *en route* gave their few remaining leaves a luminous quality, shining amber, rust and gold. Hugh began to feel more cheerful and positive about the expedition. The naked hedgerows were topped with the silver-grey of old man's beard, providing the perfect foil for jutting berries of orange and red. By the time he stopped to take advantage of a discreet lay-by not too far from Okeminster Hugh's spirits were lifted. Nearly there now, he thought. As he approached a hedge his gaze was met by the dull eye of a black-faced sheep munching in the adjacent field. The sheep regarded him with ill-disguised contempt and slowly wandered off.

The small town of Okeminster, which lay on a plain surrounded by low hills, was dominated by the tall square tower of the fifteenth-century parish church of St John.

Hugh drove carefully over the narrow bridge on the outskirts and up towards the Market Square and his destination, the Bear Hotel. The square was in fact roughly triangular, with the main road running through it and parking on either side. He parked close to the hotel by the remains of a market cross and in front of a shop proudly proclaiming the addition of goat's milk to the range of goods on offer. Dutifully obeying the order to pay and display Hugh was putting his ticket on the dashboard when he heard a commotion on the other side of the square. He locked the car, waited for a gap in the traffic and crossed the road to have a better look.

A small but vociferous group of women, some with buggies, were assembled outside the post office in the corner of the square. Off this corner led Church Lane, St John's clearly visible in the background. The group were chanting slogans, replicated on the placards held by several of its members: "Stop the Mast Madness", "Health before Wealth", "God not Mammon". Prominent amongst the protesters was an elderly but apparently robust woman with striking red-gold hair. Her voice was particularly loud and clear. She let it be known with no hint of ambiguity that she and her colleagues were unimpressed by the suggestion of a member of the local constabulary that they should move along and stop causing an obstruction. Things quietened down a bit when she was called upon to give an interview to the local press, at which point Hugh returned to the car to pick up his case.

"Bit of excitement in the square," he said to the receptionist as he checked in at the Bear.

"They're protesting against the mast some mobile phone firm wants to put on top of the church tower," said the matronly woman behind the desk. "Trying to get people to boycott church services, writing to the Bishop and all and sundry. They've been there every day this week."

"A great mast will look pretty intrusive, won't it?"

"The mobile phone people say you won't be able be see it at all. Hidden within the tower in some way. There was a meeting in the church hall to explain all about it. The vicar and the PCC – that's the Parochial Church Council – are all in favour. The church desperately needs the money. It's in a right old state. That's why they launched the preservation appeal last year."

"What's the problem, then? Sounds like rather a windfall," said Hugh, signing the register.

"The protesters say the mast's a threat to children's health. There's a Sunday school in the church hall and it's used during the week by a mother and toddler group. The mobile phone company said there won't be any risk because they'll be operating in accordance with international guidelines, whatever that means. Anyway, now the town council has come out against it as well."

"What happens next in the great mast saga?"

"Some more local consultation. Then if the mobile phone company and the PCC still want to go ahead there has to be a proper application to the district council for the planning and the diocese has to agree too."

"Sounds like it will run and run. Room 3, was it?"

"Up the stairs and first on the right after the fire door. See you later, Mr Mallard."

"Er, Mullion," said Hugh, concealing his irritation beneath an affable exterior.

Case in one hand and key in the other, he negotiated the fire door with some difficulty and gained entry to his room at only the third attempt. The room looked on to a paved courtyard in which some cast iron garden furniture was distributed, apparently at random. A girl was sitting at a small table. He put her in her mid-twenties. She was surrounded by books and magazines. Some were open and some were closed. He could see her writing furiously on a thick pad of paper. He strained to have a better look but her back was half-turned to him.

The walls of the courtyard and, it seemed, of the hotel itself were covered in ivy. It was in flower and he noticed with some surprise that the flowers just outside his window were covered in wasps. They were moving slowly and with great concentration. Through gaps in the buildings of the town he could make out the surrounding hills, bathed in warm afternoon sunshine.

Hugh finished his unpacking and turned his attention to the modest desk in the corner. The drawer yielded no more than a single sheet of hotel notepaper, an envelope and a Bible, placed there by the Gideons. A brown folder on the desk held greater promise. Lying on the bed, he opened a packet of shortbread fingers he had found by the kettle, and prepared to study the menu and a selection of leaflets on local attractions.

After an excellent meal in the hotel dining room, Hugh was looking forward to sinking into a comfortable armchair in the sitting room cum bar and flicking through the piles of local magazines and guides he had seen when he arrived. An afternoon wandering round the town had left him rather tired. He had resisted the temptations of the local museum and steered clear of the church, in case the mast protestors were still abroad. On the other hand, the purchase of a small Worcester jug in Okeminster Antiques was, he felt, clearly a necessary contribution to the local economy. His plans for the evening were, however, thrown off course by the entry into the sitting room of a gaggle of middle managers. They hailed from the West Midlands, by the sound of it. This group, it turned out, formed the advance guard of their company's awayday on 'The Role of Communication in Managing Change', to be held in the hotel's newly refurbished function room on the coming Monday. A group dinner was arranged for Sunday night. Between lagers there was much loud talk of flipcharts and overheads, white boards and post-it notes, and who would get off with Sharon if she ran true to form.

Hugh was unable to concentrate on an illustrated account of the manufacture of Blue Vinny in the

November issue of *Wessex Life*. He left the room a trifle ostentatiously and loitered in the hall. He didn't want to go back to his own room and spend the rest of the evening there and he didn't want to traipse round looking for a quiet pub, even assuming such a place could be found in Okeminster on a Saturday night. He settled for the White Hart, right next door to the Bear.

Quiet it was not. The larger of the two bars contained a dartboard, a billiard table, a fruit machine and a television screen of enormous dimensions. Apart from a couple of hard wooden chairs to one side the bar was bereft of furniture. It was full of Okeminster youth, drinking, smoking and shouting but apparently in good humour. Hugh headed for the smaller bar, in which there were a few round tables and low stools with red plush tops. There were four similar but taller stools by the bar itself. The walls were adorned with brasses and sepia photographs of bygone Okeminster.

As Hugh approached the bar a yelp of pain came from the floor. He had trodden on the tail of a collie lying half under its owner's stool. Hugh apologised profusely and wondered what to have to drink.

"You're not from round these parts, are you?" observed Sid, the collie man. "Not buying a second home, I hope. It's hard enough for young people to afford a house round here as it is."

"No. I'm just visiting." He turned to the barman, a large red-faced man wearing a checked viyella shirt. The sweat stains under his armpits reminded Hugh of maps of Cyprus. "Do you have any, um, ale?" he asked, forgoing his usual glass of red wine.

"I don't think we have any Um ale, do we, Doris?"

"No, we're right out of Um ale tonight, Harry. What's it to be? Curate's Winkle, Spotted Snake or Bouncing Bobbin?"

"A half of Spotted Snake would be fine, thank you," said Hugh stiffly.

"Don't mind us. Only teasing," said Doris. "We haven't been here long ourselves. We only took the place over eighteen months ago. I'm not sure we're really accepted yet." She handed Hugh a glass of foaming ale.

"Could you get some more peanuts from the back, please, Doris?" said Harry. "Salted and dry roasted." To Hugh he said, "There's a space over there at the table in the corner. Mind the dog."

As Hugh sat down on the diminutive stool a girl looked up from her book. She had honey-coloured shoulder-length hair and brown eyes. Hugh never could resist brown eyes. It was the first thing he had noticed about Kate at that party of Nick's in Muswell Hill.

"Hello," he said. "I saw you in the courtyard this afternoon. Next door at the hotel. I'm Hugh, by the way."

"Hi. I'm Sophie." She closed her book and placed it beside the small bottle of something green which stood half-full in front of her. Hugh glanced at the book. Hm. *Mansfield Park*. Pity I've never read it, he thought. Have to talk about something else.

"What brings you to Okeminster?" he asked, studying

Sophie's peach and cream striped jumper with some care.

"I'm here to do research on rural issues for *The World Today*."

"The programme with Raymond Hicks?"

"That's the one."

"Is that his real hair?"

"God no. He's as bald as a coot."

Hugh took a gulp of his Snake. Sophie took a swig from her bottle.

"You seemed very busy with your books in the courtyard," said Hugh. "Do you always work on a Saturday afternoon?"

"Only if I have to when I'm on an assignment. There's a lot to cover and not much time to meet my deadline."

"You don't do all your research from books, do you?"

"I comb through local newspapers and magazines, make contacts with local organisations, and so on. I was talking to people around the place yesterday. Okeminster used to be a thriving market town, apparently. Not now. There are hardly any jobs and a lot of people are commuting to other places."

"There's still a market, isn't there? I saw a poster about one on Fridays."

"That's just a small one here in the square," said Sophie. "There used to be a big livestock market down by the old station but that closed years ago. They've been arguing ever since what to do with the site. It's just a car park at the moment."

Hugh bought another round.

"So what are *you* doing in Okeminster?" asked Sophie. Hugh talked about finding the blue book, the note inside it and tracking down Dorothy.

"You make it sound like a mission," said Sophie.

"The words in the note kept going round in my head, like tunes do sometimes. I couldn't get them out of my mind. I wanted to know what they meant. Finding Dorothy seemed to be the key as the note was in her writing."

"You were certainly persistent."

"I don't give up easily. Maybe I got a bit carried away."

"Do you always get what you want?" said Sophie, lowering her eyelids momentarily.

Hugh became vaguely aware of a telephone ringing in the background.

"Oi," bawled Harry, pulling a pint of Curate's Winkle. "Phone for you."

"For me? But nobody knows I'm here."

"You are Hugh Mullion, I presume?"

"Yes, but…"

"Phone's in the passage between this bar and the other one."

The passage smelt unpleasantly of beer and disinfectant. Hugh's foot caught the corner of a large box of cheese and onion crisps. He fell heavily against a machine dispensing, he noticed with some distaste, condoms flavoured variously mint chocolate, blackcurrant, and rhubarb and custard. He picked up the dangling receiver.

"Hello. Hugh Mullion speaking."

"Ah, Hugh. It's Dorothy Johnson here. I tracked you down through your Kate and the Bear next door. Olive Snook on the desk spotted where you were going. I just wanted to say that I may be a little bit late getting back tomorrow morning. We're protesting at the church in Okeminster before, during and after the 10.30 service. Parish Communion. You may already have heard about our mast campaign. If not, I can tell you all about it tomorrow. Come at twelve anyway and George can ply you with sherry."

Dorothy rang off and Hugh returned to the bar. Sophie was no longer there. As he sat down he saw a note under his glass. He read the note, drained his glass and went back to the hotel.

21

The village of Newton FitzPosset was a couple of miles to the south west of Okeminster. The narrow road, with the occasional passing place, was lined with hazel, leaves still in place but now largely turned to yellow. A cock pheasant looked at Hugh indignantly and strutted across the road. St Mary's, off to the left as he came into the village, was an altogether more modest affair than St John's. Where St John's rose high from its mound resplendent in golden stone, St Mary's skulked squat and grey in the dark company of yews. The scattered gravestones, blotched with lichen, looked diseased.

There was no sign of life in Newton this Sunday morning. The main street was deserted. The wooden bus shelter by the junction with School Lane stood empty, its advertisements for coffee mornings and Christmas Bazaar in the village hall flapping unread. Hugh drove slowly through the village, past the general store and post office displaying posters and videos about a boy wizard, until he came to the Startled Ox. He turned right down Bell Lane and looked out for Bell Cottage.

And there it was. A square house, set well back from the road, banded warmly in brick and flint, dormers protruding from the slate roof. To the left was what Hugh took to be a garage. Set above the apex of the garage roof, just over the doors, was a large black bell. The doors themselves were the same green-blue as the front door of the house. As he went up the steps, brushing past purple hebes in the last flush of flower, he saw a man raking leaves into piles on the lawn. Slightly stooping perhaps but pretty agile for a man past eighty.

Hugh swallowed. "Hello," he said. "I'm Hugh Mullion. You must be George Johnson."

"I am indeed," said George, removing the pipe from his mouth and the twig from his full head of grey hair. "Nice to meet you." He shook Hugh by the hand. "I hope Dorothy won't be too long. I'll just go round the side and take off these boots and let you in through the front door."

In the hall, Hugh put the blue book next to a vase of Michaelmas daisies on the mahogany card table on the left-hand side. George took delivery of the wine Hugh had brought and led him into the sitting room opposite. Sipping his dry fino, Hugh looked at the red walls in the gaps between the numerous pictures and admired the antiques clustered on every surface. The French ormolu clock on the mantelpiece had stopped at ten to three. George returned with a gin and tonic for himself and offered Hugh some pistachio nuts.

"Very enterprising of you to find us," said George, inviting Hugh to sit down. "Dorothy showed me your letter. We came here about twenty years ago when I retired. I was in the heady world of investment banking. Our friends thought we were mad to leave Surrey and our children were none too pleased. Said it was irresponsible to move further away from them at our time of life." George showed no sign of remorse.

"Why did you move?" said Hugh, removing the shell from a nut with some difficulty. He put the shell in the dish on the table beside him.

"We both thought it was better to make the break and do something different while we still had our faculties than spend the rest of our lives in Surrey watching people we knew fall by the wayside, and getting frustrated and depressed when we couldn't do the things we used to do."

"Must have been rather a wrench, though."

"It was, after thirty years in the same place. But we'd been to Dorset several times before and knew the county quite well. We wanted a village rather than a town but not one that was too isolated. Newton has grown since we arrived. There are several small new estates tucked away on what was farmland when we got here. Not at all bad, actually. Traditional building styles, thatch and so on. Just need some hollyhocks and a goose girl or two."

"Sounds very Helen Allingham," said Hugh.

George smiled. "That's one of hers over there by the door to the conservatory. The picture on the left. Picked it up at a car boot sale while we were still in Surrey. That was when boot sales were just getting under way and people had no idea what they were selling. We did rather well in those days. Dorothy always did have an eye for a bargain. She's dabbled in antiques for years."

"Professionally?"

"She worked in an antique shop at one time. Books, pictures and furniture were my thing. We used to have a stall – or rather 'unit', as they called it – at the William Barnes' Antique Centre in Okeminster. It was in the disused chapel in East Street. Eventually, it got a bit much for us and we gave it up but we still do the odd fair."

"I didn't notice it when I was wandering around the town yesterday."

"It's closed now. Been converted into flats."

Suddenly, a car screeched to a halt in the gravel drive. The car door slammed.

"Stirling Moss is back," said George.

As Hugh stood up he could see through the window the woman with red-gold hair he had spotted in the Market Square the previous day. She came through the front door, dumped coat and bag in the hall, glanced in the mirror and took a deep breath as she entered the sitting room.

"Ah, Hugh, we meet at last. Has George been looking after you?"

Hugh braced himself for a firm and vigorous

handshake. It was unexpectedly light and gentle. He admired her moss-green silk shirt and well cut black trousers but, of course, said nothing as is often the way, even with women men know well.

"Much turmoil at the church this morning," said Dorothy, as George passed her a glass of sherry. "Most satisfactory. We persuaded several people to boycott the service and berated that craven vicar as he came out at the end. Betty Legg threw a mouldy clementine at him, shouting, 'You can run but you can't hide, Dr Primrose.' Apparently, we could be heard all through the service." Dorothy grinned mischievously. "Whether the PCC will change their minds is another matter."

"Don't they usually do what the vicar wants?" said George.

"We're going to work on them one by one," said Dorothy, joining Hugh on the settee. "I've got a little list. We'll start with the churchwarden, Nigel Darling. I'm sure he never would be missed. Have you heard about our mast campaign, Hugh?"

"I was briefed at the hotel yesterday," he said, omitting to mention that he had seen Dorothy in the square.

"Excellent. Word is spreading. I can't think why people want mobile phones. They merely encourage dangerous driving and delinquent behaviour. I see more and more people wandering around apparently talking to themselves. Closer inspection reveals a mobile phone, or 'mobile' as they insist on calling them, for some unknown reason."

"I suppose it's shorter and simpler," said George.

"Is it really necessary to treat adjectives as nouns just to save people the trouble of an extra word? Sheer laziness. Same with the remote control. That's gone the way of all flesh. I've even heard our own grandchildren refer to the 'remote'. Not in this house, thank you very much."

"How's your campaign progressing?" asked Hugh quickly.

"We've now got the backing of CAMM – the Campaign Against Mast Madness. We put up our MP, Sir Melbury Bubb, to write to the Secretary of State but he just got back some waffle from a junior minister saying she couldn't intervene in individual cases. Fat lot of use. Has anyone seen Mr Tibbs?"

"Last seen curled up on the towels in the laundry basket," said George. "I didn't have the heart to move him."

"I'd better go and think about lunch. Offer Hugh some more sherry," said Dorothy, leaving the room.

"Phew! Passive isn't the word that comes to mind, is it?" said George, when Dorothy was safely out of earshot.

"She obviously feels strongly about the matter."

"I find it's best to keep my head down and not argue. Years of experience. Dorothy likes a cause. Her last one was the supermarket they wanted to put on the site of the old livestock market in Okeminster. That went to a public inquiry after the council had turned it down. Dorothy performed rather well at it, I must say."

"What was the outcome?"

"The Inspector turned the proposal down too. Said it would generate too much traffic and damage trade in the town centre. I'm not so sure she's going to win on the mast, though, just between ourselves."

"Rather splendid hair, if I may say so."

"What? Oh, Dorothy's. Assisted these days, of course, but the colour is much as it was when I first knew her after the War. The landlord of the flat she had then called her Beata Beatrix, after the Rossetti painting."

"The GIs used to call it strawberry blond," said Dorothy, coming back into the room wearing a striped apron. "But that's another story. Would you like to come next door?"

The panelled dining room felt dingy after the exuberance of the other room. Hugh sat facing a portrait of a woman in mourning. 1850-something, he guessed. Her soft eyes were tinged with melancholy. She seemed to be looking right at him.

"Do have a roll." Dorothy passed Hugh the basket. "I hope there are no foreign bodies, unlike the last lot we got from the bakers in the square."

"Reminds me of that Gogol short story," said George. "Chap found a nose in his roll. It went round St Petersburg in a uniform and plumed hat. I don't think Okeminster's quite ready for a peripatetic nose."

"It could only do a better job than that Nigel Darling. Anyway, Hugh, I should thank you for your letter. Very clever of you to track me down."

"It was more thanks to Colin Smedley and his wife Alison. I gather he used to live next door to you."

"Good God," said Dorothy through a mouthful of crab. "Colin Smedley married. I suppose he would be by now. I never entirely cared for the Smedleys. Not quite our sort. As for Norman Smedley. Dreadful little man. Had halitosis and a Hillman Minx."

"That's going back a bit," said George. "Their last car was a Fiat."

"He kept coming round to use our phone. Whenever we saw him we shouted 'fish knives' to each other as a warning and pretended to be out."

"There was absolutely nothing wrong with the Smedleys' phone. Norman just wanted an excuse to see Dorothy. And who can blame him?"

"What an appalling thought. Mind you, the kids got on all right with the young Smedleys. They were always in and out. I always felt rather sorry for Mrs Smedley. Hermione. The name never quite suited her. She tried very hard with the Fairview Players but wasn't really up to it. Talk about coarse acting. She could never remember her lines and used the same facial expression for every emotion."

"I gather you were a bit of a thespian yourself," said Hugh.

Dorothy stiffened slightly. "I like to think I played my part. In every sense."

"Dorothy was a leading light in the Fairview Players," said George, a note of pride in his voice. "Her Antigone was talked about for months afterwards. Rave reviews in the local papers."

"People I didn't know from Adam kept coming up to me in the fish shop and the greengrocer's and greeting me like a long-lost friend. Funny how when people see you on stage they expect you to know them too."

"Have you been tempted to tread the boards, Hugh?" asked George.

"No. I don't think I could. Not in front of lots of people. I'd get hopelessly tongue-tied. It's bad enough when I have to speak at conferences."

"It's surprising what you can do when you set your mind to it," said Dorothy. "Very surprising." There was an oddly determined note in her voice that made Hugh feel uneasy. "What about school plays?"

"I helped paint scenery under close supervision," he said, draining his glass of Sancerre.

"Lamb with garlic – and rosemary, for remembrance. And here's Mr Tibbs. Awoken from his slumbers by the smell of lunch. I'm afraid you're too late for the crab." Dorothy was addressing a sleek tabby cat with over-long whiskers, which was giving every impression of not having been fed for a month. As she bent down her gold locket brushed the top of Mr Tibbs' head. "You're a beautiful pussy, aren't you? Yes, you are. Have you had an exhausting morning being asleep? This is Hugh. He's come all the way from London. I don't know if he likes cats."

"I do. I'm great friends with Kipling, my father's cat. And I talk to cats on walls and in the garden when I think no one's looking."

"Don't you have a cat of your own?"

"Kate says we can't as we're both out all day."

"I can't see that's a problem if you put in a cat flap. I don't hold with litter trays myself. If you want a cat I should just get one if I were you."

Mr Tibbs let it be known that he could tolerate lamb with garlic, even though he preferred it without. George cut off a bit surreptitiously and headed towards the kitchen. Mr Tibbs shot after him.

"Tell me about Michael and Jennifer," said Hugh after George had returned.

"You are well informed," said George, pouring the claret.

"Colin Smedley, no doubt," said Dorothy. "I don't suppose he mentioned that he once tried to persuade Jennifer to remove her knickers in the woodshed for a Milky Bar and a packet of Spangles."

"Strangely, no. Did he succeed?"

"Certainly not. They were mint Spangles and she only liked the fruit ones. Michael and Jennifer both live in south London. Not all that far from you, actually. Michael is a civil servant, I regret to say. Still, every family has its black sheep. Rather a disappointment. We had hoped he'd do a proper job."

"He's done quite well," said George. "Director of something at the Ministry of... .What is it?"

"I can never remember. They keep changing the name. Michael's married to Jane," said Dorothy. "She's a management consultant. They have two children. Jennifer and Stephen can't. Not for want of trying but there we are. At least we can put everyone up if they all decide to descend on us at the same time."

"What do they do?"

"Jennifer teaches French at the local school and Stephen's in computers. He has tried to explain what he does. Which would you like first: cheese or the last syllabub of recorded time?"

After lunch, Hugh took a turn round the garden with Dorothy while George retreated to his workshop.

"The fig's looking rather sad without its leaves," she said. "You should see it in the summer."

"Do you get many figs from it?"

"The ripest ones are at the top and the starlings usually beat us to it. That buddleia was absolutely smothered with red admirals and small tortoiseshells this year. There's an awful lot of cutting back and tidying up still to be done all round the garden. A boy from the village comes and helps with that."

"I like the urn," said Hugh, pointing to the ornament by the gate through to the orchard. "Is there only one?"

"We picked it up cheap somewhere, covered in rust. George cleaned it up and painted it black. Just the one. There's something rather appealing about asymmetry in a garden, don't you think? Too much balance can look contrived. Things don't have to come in pairs."

"I suppose not. But some things are made to go together, aren't they? Like shoes or vases. Are you still involved in plays? I saw a poster in the town for a production by the Okeminster Amateur Dramatic Society."

"*Dancing at Lughnasa*. The OADS did it very well. But we haven't done anything on that front ourselves since we left Surrey. To be honest, it was just beginning to get a little bit much for both of us, though we never let on. And neither of us could face starting all over again with a new society."

"OADS reminds me of OUDS. Did you act while you were at Oxford?"

"What? Oxford? No. I mean, yes. Sorry. It wasn't in the forefront of my mind. It was such a long time ago. Must be a good sixty years at least."

Hugh noticed a distant sadness in Dorothy's pale grey eyes. It could have been nostalgia.

"Let's go and have a cup of tea," she said. She seemed troubled by the reminder of the past.

"I don't normally do this at this time of day," said Dorothy later. "More a two o'clock in the morning thing and George isn't really a fan. But I'm in the mood."

"Are you often in circulation at two o'clock in the morning?"

"When I can't sleep I seek solace in a glass of whisky and a game of patience. I keep the cards in the drawer of the canterbury. Sometimes I fall asleep in front of the television and wake up during some ghastly breakfast programme. Such awful people. All those fake tans and split infinitives."

Dorothy put on the CD. "Ah, Miles," said Hugh.

"Excellent." But Dorothy was staring silently through the sitting room window into the gloaming beyond. Marjorie wouldn't approve, thought Hugh: 'Summertime' in November.

"It's hardly a summer evening on Catfish Row," said Dorothy after a while. "But the music has a peculiarly wistful quality that seems right in the dying moments of an autumn day. George and I saw *Porgy and Bess* at the Stoll Theatre in Kingsway. Must have been half a century ago."

As Hugh was about to go he saw the blue book on the hall table. "I nearly forgot to give you this," he said, handing the book to Dorothy.

She stared at it silently. "I never thought I'd see that again," she said after a moment. She flicked slowly through the book. "I was having a clear-out before we left our house in Surrey. It must have got into the box of books I gave to Hermione Smedley. It was a mistake."

"You wrote your name in pencil in all the books."

"I never write my name in ink. George gets very cross when people do that in books."

"Except in *The Portrait of a Lady*."

"Oh, did I?" said Dorothy. She glanced at the flyleaf. "So I did. Well, that was before I knew George." She darted into the room opposite the sitting room and came back holding Volume I. "Reunited at last," she said.

"A pair, in fact."

Dorothy smiled. "Don't forget to take the bag of Bramleys. Keep in touch. You must come again with

Kate. I'd like to meet her. I'm rather interested in homeopathy."

George reappeared wiping his hands on a rag that had once been white. "Have a safe journey," he said. "When you come again you must see my workshop."

22

*W*hat did you think?" said George, joining Dorothy in the sitting room shortly afterwards. "You look tired."

"I need a drink," she said, flopping into an armchair. She wedged a small rectangular cushion between herself and the side of the chair. "I found some of that disgusting suze in the back of the cupboard this morning. It looks revolting and tastes even worse. I thought we'd got rid of it years ago. I can't think why you bought it."

"*You* bought it because you liked the colour."

"I must have had an off day. How can gentian liqueur be bright yellow? Reminds me of that specimen I gave to Dr Whatshisname."

"Sherry?"

"Andrews, wasn't it?"

"Fino or amontillado?" asked George, arms akimbo.

"He seemed a nice boy."

"Hardly a boy, dear. He must be…what would you say?"

"Amontillado."

"Early- to mid-thirties?" hazarded George.

"Something like that. Rather good-looking."

"If you say so, dear."

"I could see him in a white linen suit, lounging on a rug on a long hot summer afternoon before the First World War."

"You were in two minds about answering his letter when you first read it." George put two glasses of sherry on the small round table between Dorothy's chair and the settee.

"Yes but I'm glad I did. Intriguing to meet someone who went to all that trouble to find me. It wouldn't have been the same just asking him to send the book."

"Do we have any peanuts?"

"There's a box of those cheesy things I got from Truckles."

"I'm still not clear why he did go to all that effort," said George, hovering.

"I'm not sure either. He said he wanted to see if I had the missing volume."

"Bit of a long shot. Why should he care? But what other reason could there be?"

"He was quieter than I expected, considering he must be pretty determined."

"He hadn't met you before. You can be a bit overpowering."

"I thought I was quite well behaved."

George went to the kitchen in search of cheesy things. Dorothy gripped the arm of her chair as she bent down to pick up the wood shavings that had detached themselves from the elbow of George's sweater. She felt faint as she sat back up. She thought again about Hugh's visit. She rather admired his detective work. But there had to be more to it than returning a long-lost book, didn't there? She had nearly let her guard slip once or twice. I'd had better be more careful next time, she thought.

23

*H*ugh was ordering an obscure book from a dealer in New Hampshire when the front door bell rang.

"I'll get it," called Kate.

He completed the transaction, switched off the computer and went downstairs to the sitting room.

"How's Mullion of the Yard?" said Sue, giving him a squeeze. He reciprocated tentatively and straightened the shade of the standard lamp. The fringe swayed provocatively. Kate was now shouting into a mobile phone in the kitchen. "Met your mysterious Dark Lady, I hear."

"I don't know about dark," he said, signalling to Sue to sit down. He leaned against the mantelpiece and studied the pattern in the rug for a moment before looking up. "I'm not sure what to make of her. She terrorises local clerics and faceless bureaucrats. Keen sense of public duty. Or perhaps she just wants something to do. Or to take her mind off...I don't know. Anyway, the long-suffering George takes refuge in his workshop and restores furniture. Still, you know what they say about opposite poles."

"She sounds rather a dragon."

"A bit fierce at first sight, perhaps, but I think she has a soft centre. She's pretty gooey about cats and says I should get one. Maybe I shall."

"Kate said something about antiques and pictures."

"Everywhere. They've got some very nice things. I was sorely tempted."

"You didn't!"

"Certainly not," he said, with mock indignation. "Dorothy likes Miles Davis too."

"Lucky you've got things in common. Aren't Dorothy and George nearly antiques themselves?"

"They're pretty well preserved."

"That was Linda," said Kate, coming back into the room. "She's at her wits' end. Says her daughter has become a witch and joined a coven called the Silver Cauldron. It all came out when Emma and her friend got back from a witchfest in Croydon, of all places."

"I always knew there was more to Croydon than met the eye," said Hugh. "Is there a cure for witchcraft? A remedy of great potency?"

"It's called being grounded. Emma has to come straight back from school each day and isn't allowed out without a parent until further notice."

"Chained to a moody teenage witch. Not my idea of fun. Have you ever been attracted to the wicca way, Sue?"

"God, no. I'm not being put up the duff by the Lord of Misrule, thank you very much. I'm not that desperate. And think of all those hooves. I'm wondering about becoming a born-again virgin."

"Isn't that rather closing the stable door?"

"Hugh!"

"That's all right," said Sue. "It's more like wiping the slate clean and saving myself for Mister Right. True love waits, they say. Anyway, the chastity movement is quite big in America, I read somewhere. They've got slogans like 'Stop your urgin', be a virgin'."

"Pardon me while I vomit," said Hugh, falling to his knees and pretending to retch horribly. As he did so, a small piece of paper dropped onto the rug from the top pocket of his shirt. "A timely distraction. This is the note we found in the Henry James. I took it out before I gave the book to Dorothy to remind me to mention it to her. I forgot."

"I thought that was why you went," said Sue. "To find out what the note meant."

"Partly. But I got so wrapped up in Johnson history and reminiscence that it slipped my mind. I was halfway to Okeminster by the time I remembered. Dorothy's a pretty over-powering presence."

"Here we go again," said Kate. "Could you give it a rest. I'm beginning to wonder if there's something between you and Dorothy." She gave Sue a wink.

"Hardly. She's old enough to be my mother. In fact, a lot older than my mother is…was…would have been."

Hugh said no more about the visit. All the same, he wondered if Dorothy herself had remembered the note. Not very likely after all this time.

24

*H*ugh stared out of the window of his office at the wet roofs below. He looked at the posters of historic buildings on his walls and at the postcards pinned to his board. He contemplated the neat labels on the drawers of his filing cabinets. He was supposed to be working on his paper on the Dutch approach to conservation of historic buildings through better maintenance. It was due to be circulated shortly to members of the Commission's conservation policy sub-committee. His heart was not in it. His secretary, Belinda, came in to remind him of the eleven o'clock meeting with Roger and other staff in the Directorate.

"Oh God. What's it about?"

Belinda opened the diary. "It says here: 'Changing the culture and improving working practices'. Apparently, we've got to work smarter not harder and get more bangs for the buck. Sounds disgusting."

"How long will it last?"

"Sheila says an hour at the most."

"Should be over in two, then."

Belinda turned to go. "Oh, Hugh," she said, pointing to his screen. "Red nine on the black ten."

He was about to leave for Roger's meeting when the telephone rang.

"Hi. It's Sophie."

"How are you? Sorry. I mean, this is a bit of a bad moment. I'm already late for a meeting. Did you get back all right on Sunday?"

"I'm fine," said Sophie calmly. "So was the journey, apart from a hailstorm near Andover. Why don't we have lunch? You can tell me all about your Dorothy expedition."

"Er, when…?"

"How about next Tuesday?"

"Let's see," said Hugh, consulting his diary. "That looks all right."

"One o'clock, Liberty's café?"

"See you then."

Hugh was shaking as he picked up a folder of papers and left the room. He felt much as he had when the bidding started for the picture at Gavels. Perhaps he was coming down with flu. He vaguely wondered if it wise to see Sophie again. Still, lunch couldn't hurt, could it?

25

On Saturday morning Hugh clinked into Toad Books on his way back from Bin Ends.

"Peel me a grape," said Charlie.

"Please. Remember your manners," said Anthony, peeling the parrot a grape. "You're quite capable of doing it yourself, you idle bird." Charlie cocked his head and looked quizzical.

"You can see who's in charge round here," Marjorie said to Hugh. "Mr Buffo brought him back one of those compact discs. *Anything Goes*. I ask you."

"You did tell me Charlie was a Cole Porter bird."

"He's learning to whistle along," said Anthony, wiping his hands on the large spotted handkerchief produced with a flourish from his right pocket, rather in the manner of a conjurer. "I thought of you, Hugh, when I was in Washington Square. Henry James and all that. Not that he lived there. He was born just off it, I think. Not quite James' ideal of quiet and of genteel retirement these days. More acrobats and skateboarders and people walking their dogs."

"What were you doing in New York?" said Hugh, depositing his bags with a clunk by the remainder table.

"Oh, just business," said Anthony, airily.

"Books?"

"A few but they're heavy to bring back. Picked up some bargains in that big bookstore in Fulton Street, not far from the fish market."

"I've never been to New York," said Hugh.

"Nor have I," put in Marjorie.

"Well, there are plenty of cheap flights."

"Stayed in some smart hotel, I suppose," said Marjorie, spinning unexpectedly in her chair.

"No, I was in an apartment in SoHo, staying with a friend."

"He's wearing the Prado shirt he bought." It sounded like an accusation.

"I think you mean Prada," said Anthony. "The Prado is a museum in Madrid."

"Sorry, I'm sure. Some of us can't run to designer clothes," said Marjorie, tugging at the cardigan draped around her shoulders. It had large strawberries embroidered on the pockets. "Cost an arm and a leg, I daresay."

"On the contrary, it was very reasonable. I got it in a little shop in the East Village that specialises in previously owned designer wear."

"Previously owned? You don't mean…second-hand?"

"I do but so what?"

"Well, really. Some of us have our standards," said Marjorie, retreating to the kitchen with a brace of mugs for replenishment.

"You missed the auction, Hugh," said Anthony. "Books this month."

"I was in Dorset on the only day I could have been to the viewing. Volume II of *The Portrait of a Lady* is now with its rightful owner."

"I'm glad it's back home at last. Lucky I didn't chuck it out. I got some nice Rackhams at the auction, not to mention a couple of early Iris Murdochs, some P G Wodehouse and the Gormenghast trilogy – all in dustwrappers and signed by the lad himself. Mervyn Peake. Not a bad haul." Anthony looked smug.

"I wish I'd been there," said Hugh ruefully. He was leaning against the remainder table, his hand on a biography of an early Victorian poet. "I see you've made a lot of progress with clearing out those rooms." Both the green doors to the right at the back of the shop were open. "They're really quite big. I didn't expect much more than overgrown cupboards. Why don't you knock them together to make one large room? You could put in a few spotlights, slap on some white emulsion, and use it as an exhibition space for local artists. I've seen it done elsewhere."

"That's not a bad idea," said Anthony. "It's only a plaster board partition between them and the carpet's all right. Next thing you'll be suggesting I open a café as well."

"Perhaps just a discreet coffee percolator or two at

this stage." Hugh had a thought. "Do you remember our neighbour, Lucy Potter? She paints. You came to her Christmas show last year."

26

*I*t was the first Sunday in December. Hugh was attending a conference on historic towns in Exeter the following morning. He thought he would take advantage of being in that general part of the world to pop in and see Dorothy and George at Bell Cottage. He might learn something more. Anyway, he liked them. He had remembered to bring the note. Now he just had to produce it at the right moment.

"Can I press you to a slice of cinnamon toast?" asked Dorothy as Hugh put his case down in the hall.

"That takes me back. I haven't had cinnamon toast for years. My mother used to make it."

"It's very easy. You or Kate could do it. I'm sorry she wasn't able to come."

"She's seeing her parents and I'm just passing through. Nice of George to come all that way to pick me up, particularly as…"

"No, he's not getting any younger. He's fine driving during the day but I don't let him out in the dark any more. Our son, Michael, will take you back to the station on his way home."

"Michael? Is he here?"

"Yes, he came down yesterday. Brought a chair for George to do something with. He's ensconced in the study with a laptop at the moment." Dorothy put a finger to her lips and pointed to the door on the left. The vase on the card table beside it now contained an arrangement of dried flowers. "Some panic about revising his draft delivery plan before the Treasury see it. All Greek to me."

"He has my deepest sympathy."

Dorothy took Hugh down the hall and hung up his coat on one of the hooks outside the kitchen door. The kitchen was warm and smelled of lunch.

"Michael's is the car parked outside in the lane though why he needs a Range Rover in south London I can't imagine. I don't think the roads have degenerated that far, even there. If I'd thought, I could have asked him to give you a lift down. Pity you can't stay the night."

"I have an early start tomorrow and the organisers have booked me a room at the conference hotel."

A tortoiseshell cat was winding through Hugh's legs, purring loudly. Dorothy picked her up and presented her to him. "This is Minnie, stealer of cheese and anything else that gets left out. Only last week she ran off with the Stinking Bishop. Say hello to Hugh, Minnie."

He gently shook her right paw. "Why Minnie?"

"Short for Minnie the Minx. It took us a while to decide what to call her. Nothing seemed quite right."

"George," said Dorothy from her position on the sitting-room settee. "Have you seen my blue remembered pills? The ones I got after I saw Dr Finnis on Friday. That man is the end. Bring back Dr Andrews, I say. I'd rattle if I took everything he prescribed. He must think I'm a pushover."

"I very much doubt it, dear. They're right by you, on the top of the display cabinet."

"So they are. I went on to the district council offices afterwards and quizzed a man in the planning department. Not the one who was so co-operative about that supermarket proposal. Some pompous little man, who clearly didn't know his job.

"Not a sympathiser?"

"He tried to tell me that it wasn't the purpose of the planning system to stop things happening. Said it was a question of what was in the public interest. I made it quite clear that bombarding people with death rays from the top of the church tower was hardly in the public interest."

"What did he say to that?"

"Something incomprehensible about electro-magnetic fields and government guidance, and that if I wanted to object I was welcome to do so and my views would be taken into account. I said if development control didn't mean controlling development, what did it mean? Then I walked out."

"Poor chap," said George.

"I sometimes wonder whose side you're on. You'll have gathered, Hugh, that the mast application has been put in. If the council don't decide it in eight weeks it goes through anyway. Absolutely scandalous."

"Where does that leave the campaign?"

"We've got to get our skates on to rally the opposition and get objections in. Ted Castle has got 'Stop the Mast' posters in the windows of Motte and Bailey's and his wife Beryl is collecting signatures for the petition. She's resigned from the brass-cleaning rota at St John's. She's one of the growing band leaving the church and coming over to St Mary's in Newton."

"I didn't see much sign of life when I was here last time."

"The services rotate between three different parishes. It's St Mary's turn again this evening. Not that we're regular attenders ourselves, though I do still help out with the occasional church fete."

"That's so you can look through the bric-a-brac before anyone else," said George.

"I pay the going rate," protested Dorothy. "What about you and the books?"

The telephone rang before George could reply. "It's Jennifer," said Dorothy.

"This could take a while," said George. "Come and have a look at my workshop. The heater's on so it won't be too chilly."

Hugh followed George into the hall, past the kitchen and out through the back door. His foot caught a lone quince on the path and propelled it across the lawn. The workshop was in an outbuilding between the end of the garage and the cold frames. There were hydrangeas on either side of the door.

"Sorry about the mess," said George as he switched on the light. A naked bulb exposed a floor covered in sawdust and wood shavings. A large bookcase loomed directly in front of him, the higher shelves crammed with stains, polishes, varnishes and glues, the lower occupied by tins of paint. A couple of chairs hung over the workbench.

"It's an Aladdin's cave," said Hugh in wonderment. He pointed to another tall bookcase to the right of the door. "What's in those tins? I've never seen so many."

"Just screws and nails and things like that. Won't you sit down? Mind the two by four."

Hugh faltered, mesmerised by the display of screwdrivers, hammers and chisels clipped neatly to the wall above the bench. He sat down heavily on an old kitchen chair.

"Tell me about the Fairview Players. Dorothy said you did the sets."

"I designed and built them – with a bit of help from other members. Did some stage management and a few other things too. Even front of house if they were short. I donned an ancient double-breasted dinner jacket with the shiniest lapels you've ever seen. Wowed the ladies in the box office." George smiled enigmatically.

"No acting?"

"That was Dorothy's department. She was good, very

good, but they tended to be more character parts in later years. Then she did props. Cluttered up our garages with them. I never did know why she bought so many bunches of plastic bananas. We gave them to a jumble sale when we moved. I don't think they were entirely grateful."

"Is that how you met, through amateur dramatics?"

"We were both members of the same society in Twickenham after the war. The Mummers. We did three plays a year and the odd drama festival."

"When was that?"

"Must have been the late 'forties when we met. She was more restrained then. Quite withdrawn in some ways. Still, we seemed to get on and went to the theatre a lot together. Mostly West End. There was the Q Theatre too in those days. Opposite Kew Bridge Station. We used to go there. And to the Richmond Theatre. Coffee in the Montana Snack Bar afterwards. So many plays." George sighed.

"You certainly got about. We rarely stray beyond the National. Does anything stand out?"

"Emlyn Williams as Charles Dickens at the Lyric Hammersmith," said George without hesitation. "Late 1951. I remember that because it was the night before I proposed to Dorothy. I was sick with nerves, even though she had been hinting for a while. I pretended not to notice. We got married in 1952 and had a flat for a year or so. Then when Michael arrived we moved to Surrey."

"Dorothy stayed at home?"

"That was quite normal then. But when the children were both at school she got a job in a local antique shop for part of the time. In fact, she was working in an antique shop when I first got to know her in London so she already knew the ropes."

"Didn't she feel she was wasting an Oxford education?"

"I don't think so. Education isn't just for jobs, is it? She always said she didn't want to be a teacher or a civil servant, like so many of her contemporaries."

"So she went straight into the world of antiques?"

"I believe she was a secretary for a while but I'm a bit hazy about what she did before I met her. Dorothy's never been very forthcoming about her time at Oxford for some reason and didn't seem to keep up with people after she left."

Hugh recalled Dorothy's uneasiness when he had raised Oxford with her in the garden the first time he was here. Why was she reluctant to talk about it? Had something happened there, all those years ago?

"George. George. You'll catch your death out there. Stop boring Hugh and come inside."

"The Siren calls," said George. "She never did have any difficulty hitting the back wall."

Hugh picked up an old saw that was straddling an orange box.

"My father's," said George. Those are his initials stamped into the handle. F.E.J. Frank Ebenezer Johnson. Nice man."

*

"Jennifer was telling me about her new kitchen," said Dorothy, when they were back in the sitting room. "It's going to cost a fortune. Taking everything out and starting again. Shaker style, apparently. Maple with brushed steel handles, if you please. She's been dragging poor Stephen round south London to look at sinks and cooker hoods. And the price of the tiles. I told her she could have got them at a tenth of the cost at the Magical World of Tiles but she had to have these special French ones to go with the colour she'd chosen for the walls. People are extraordinary, aren't they?"

"Yes, dear," said George, half-suppressing a smile.

"I forgot to show you this last time," said Hugh, putting down his cup and opening his wallet. A small black and white photograph of a woman fell out and landed on the carpet. He picked it up and put it back. "My mother. I meant this," he said, producing a piece of paper. He unfolded it and gave it to Dorothy. "It was inside the blue book – the Henry James."

Dorothy looked at the note. Her eyes narrowed. She paled and went quiet for a moment. "Means nothing to me," she said, casually.

" 'D. Fear death by water.' " read George. "It's your writing, Dorothy. It looks like the same ink as in the front of the book, on the flyleaf."

"The quotation is Eliot, from *The Waste Land*, but I don't know who D is," said Hugh.

"Sounds like a warning," said George. "The only D I know is you, Dorothy. Not that I knew you in those days, of course." He gave Dorothy a look.

"I'd hardly send myself an anonymous note, would I?" said Dorothy sharply. "I'm afraid I can't shed any light on this at all."

"Time we were on our way," said Michael, coming into the room and shaking Hugh by the hand. His features were a disconcerting amalgam of Dorothy and George. His hair was dark brown, greying at the temples. Horn-rimmed glasses gave him a studious, faintly donnish, air. "I've left the Christmas pudding on the kitchen table. I got it earlier than usual this year as I happened to be in Piccadilly. You haven't forgotten where you put the sixpences?"

"Same place as usual. In the red lacquer box over there. Used to be silver threepenny bits until Michael and Jennifer spent them on ice creams," she said to Hugh. "I'd had them for years. The ice cream man was only too happy to accept them. Don't forget the Bramleys, Michael." She put the note on the mantelpiece under a small enamel snuff box.

As the car set off down the unlit road a pair of eyes shone in the headlights.

"The elusive Mr Tibbs, if I'm not mistaken," said Michael. "Aka Nimrod…"

"The mighty hunter?"

"Exactly so. He catches mice and brings them into the house. Baby birds and the occasional frog too. Leaves the remains under the kitchen table or thereabouts. Never wise to walk around the kitchen barefoot."

*

"How long have you been with the Heritage Commission?" asked Michael after an awkward silence. He turned right on to the main road, avoiding Okeminster.

"Must be about ten years now."

"Pity Sir Richard is leaving. He was rather a good thing."

"I can't see a successor in place by the time he goes."

"Most unlikely. You work with Roger Moon, I believe."

"How on earth did you know that?" said Hugh, shifting uneasily in his seat.

"Roger and I worked together some years ago. He was on secondment to the Ministry. I had lunch with him last week."

"Oh. Really?"

"He seems to think highly of you, though he thought you'd been a bit preoccupied the last few weeks."

"What with one thing and another. It's our busy period."

"My parents seem quite taken with you too."

"They've been very hospitable. They're both remarkable for their age."

"On the face of it, but I don't think either of them is as vigorous as they appear."

"They're a pretty effective double act."

"True," said Michael. He was beginning to sound more relaxed. "My mother out front making the noise, my father backstage providing the technical back-up. Actually, not just technical. She depends on him more than you might think. She's terrified of what will happen when he dies."

"What will happen?"

"She refuses to discuss it. Both Jennifer and I have tried."

"What impels her to take on the world?"

"You may well ask," Michael said slowly and with feeling. "She invents a crisis, makes a drama out of it and then takes a starring role. Even the simplest things like where to put the Golden Jubilee seat on the village green or the name of one of these new estates. She got the parish council to argue with the house builders for six months over a development of five houses." Michael was becoming more animated.

"Just over the name?"

"The builders wanted to call it Hillview. Not unreasonable since the estate backed on to a hill. The council wanted Longmead, the old name of the land it was on. Eventually, they compromised on Field Lane. I think they have a sneaking regard for her round here even if she does tend to act the Lady of the Manor."

"You didn't have a boring childhood, then."

"Boring, no." Michael hesitated. In the dark Hugh could sense words being chosen with care. "The Fairview Players rather dominated things but we were happy enough being left to our own devices. My mother's public appearances were a bit embarrassing, at least for us. She had – still has – a loud and penetrating voice that was widely mimicked by local children, particularly Colin Smedley next door."

"That he didn't mention."

"She once berated me for mumbling in the queue to see Father Christmas at Harrods with the words: 'Speak up, Michael. I want clear diction and pure vowel sounds.' Everyone turned round to look. My mother used to address withering remarks to unfortunate shop assistants with a certain…hauteur, shall I say. I doubt that anyone present has forgotten her bellowing 'Out, vile jelly' to the waitress who brought us strawberry instead of mandarin orange in The Copper Kettle."

"There's no malice in it, though," said Hugh.

"Oh, no. I'm sure of that. Just a different view of the world and what constitutes normal behaviour. I tease Jennifer that she's getting like her."

"You weren't tempted by the stage yourself?"

"Jennifer and I rather reacted against it, at least in later years. We were cajoled into hearing my mother's lines in the kitchen. We kept hoping she'd get smaller parts but she always set her face against it. Said that small parts were much more difficult than large ones."

"How's that? More to learn with large parts, surely?"

"Something about having less time to establish yourself with the audience if you're not on for long. Needing to make an impact quickly. Anyway, things were different when we were younger. My mother used to dress us up in costumes that were miles too big. She made us up as well. She had a book of make-up, I remember, with a picture of Harlequin on the cover.

And an old cigar box with sticks of make-up and lining pencils. She once spent ages making me up as a Chinaman."

"Sounds great fun. Did you see all her plays?"

"We went to most of the Fairview productions while we were there, not to mention plays put on by other local drama groups. Pantomimes at Christmas too and trips up to London to meet my father and see the lights in Oxford Street. Usually something afterwards – *Peter Pan, Treasure Island, Where the Rainbow Ends.*"

"What do your children make of her?"

"They adore her, as she does them. She and my father are both very kind to them. They love coming here and playing in the orchard. My mother says Alice looks just like her at that age. I'll take her word for it. I've never seen any pictures of my mother as a child. Odd, when you come to think of it."

The car swung into the station forecourt and deposited Hugh and his case. "You and Kate must come round for a drink," said Michael as he headed off towards the London road.

27

*D*o you know what time it is?" asked George blearily. The cord of his dressing gown trailed behind him on the sitting room carpet. "It's three o'clock in the morning," he said, not waiting for an answer.

"I couldn't sleep," said Dorothy. She was perched on the edge of a chair, Minnie curled in a tight ball on her lap. Miles Davis was playing quietly in the background. "That note brought everything back."

George was silent for a while. Then he said softly: "It was a long time ago."

"I know."

"Before I met you."

"I know."

"Are you going to tell him?"

"What for? I hardly know him. I've only met him twice."

"As you wish. Did you notice the photograph? The one of his mother."

"No. It was upside down from where I was and he picked it up pretty quickly."

"It looked like you, about the time we first came here."

"Really? How extraordinary. But he couldn't have known that when he wrote to me, if you see what I mean. I wonder if we'll meet him again."

"Why don't you come back to bed?" He lifted Minnie gently from her lap and parked the sleeping cat on the settee. Dorothy took his hand and slowly stood up. She took a few steps and steadied herself against the mantelpiece. The note under the enamel snuff box had gone.

28

*H*ugh traipsed slowly back from the station, briefcase in one hand and flowers in the other. As he approached the parade, he saw a man in blue overalls coming out of Toad Books, an aluminium stepladder balanced precariously on his left shoulder. The man secured the ladder to the roof of the van parked on the pavement, flung his tools inside, and drove off quickly in the general direction of the high street. Spiro came out of the Mini-market next door, re-arranged the paw-paws, and tested the ripeness of the melons with his large hairy hands.

Hugh stopped outside the bookshop. He was bathed in light at a time when darkness was normally to be expected.

"You're making good progress," he said, as he entered the shop.

"I'm running out of time," said Anthony, in a state of some agitation. "The exhibition opens on Saturday and we're miles behind. Charlie's very cross about the dust."

"What a transformation," said Hugh, putting the flowers on the pine table that served as a desk and his briefcase beneath it. "That room's enormous. Bright, isn't it?"

"I've just had the spots put in. I'm hoping it'll be all right once the pictures are on the walls. Otherwise, I'll have to issue dark glasses."

"Where *are* the pictures?"

Anthony pointed to a large quantity of paintings in plain wood frames stacked upright in one corner of the room.

"I see what you mean. There *are* a lot."

"Lucy and I are hanging them tomorrow. She's drawn up a plan but it's going to take ages to get them exactly right. At least she's put the numbers on. I've been delegated to do the price lists."

"Typed painstakingly on your trusty Imperial."

"On my word processor, if you don't mind."

"I didn't know Toad Books had entered the electronic age."

"Of course. How do you think I do my catalogues? Come and have a look."

He took the shop door off the snib, told Charlie where they were going, and led Hugh upstairs. At the top, the carpet gave way to worn chocolate-coloured linoleum. Boxes were piled waist high the length of the landing. Anthony moved the ironing board and opened one of the doors on the left.

"This is my office and retreat. An oasis of calm and tranquillity. I've been having a tidy-up." He ushered Hugh into the room. The walls were pale apricot. Two Caucasian rugs were on the floor.

"Good heavens. It's…"

"Not chaotic? Exudes order and efficiency whilst contriving to be warm and welcoming?"

"Exactly," said Hugh.

"I shoved most of the stuff next door and gave the room a damn good clean. I brought a few things from the house to cheer it up."

Hugh glanced at the top of the well-ordered desk. "Why do you make Marjorie answer the phone if you've got one up here?"

"The one downstairs is the shop phone. This one is my private number for other business."

Before he could probe further Hugh was distracted by a picture on the wall hanging above the computer.

"That's not a…surely…over there?"

"It is, yes. There are a couple more behind you."

"Picasso etchings! Where on earth did you get them?"

"Oh, I've had them for years," said Anthony with studied unconcern. He was more interested in showing Hugh his new printer. "Look at this. It does seventeen pages a minute. I'll run off a whole load of price lists. Lucy's bringing copies of the CV she updated for the Battersea art fair."

As he made suitably admiring noises, Hugh saw on the desk a framed photograph of a woman and a small girl. He did not recognise either of them.

A dull splash in the cold, dark water. Ripples, ever-increasing concentric circles. A piece of paper floating on the surface. Lights. Cries. Running.

Dorothy woke with a start. She was shaking and breathing heavily. She got up and drew back the curtains. The room was bathed in pale blue moonlight, throwing everything into sharp relief. George slept soundly. Perhaps she had not cried out after all.

"Relax, dear," she said to herself. "It was only a dream." Or a nightmare. She sipped at the remains of the tea in the mug on her bedside cabinet. It had lost its warmth hours ago. She put down the mug, lay back in the bed and pulled the quilt over her. The past was catching up with her, she thought. What to do next?

*H*ugh negotiated his way delicately between the bags of Maris Piper on his left and the large bucket on his right. "It's the health and safety," said the tall young man with the mop. He was resplendent in the blue and yellow uniform that distinguished members of Waitfare's staff. "We've had no end of trouble with squashed grapes. Woman in our Wimbledon store slipped on one and broke her leg. She's suing for God knows how much."

"I shall try to be vigilant," said Hugh sleepily, as he drove his trolley over the corner of the mat by the cabinet. He recognised the man from his previous visits to the supermarket. Last week Virgil (as his name badge revealed him to be) was on the nine items or fewer checkout, the week before he had been seen placing deodorants on a shelf where no one could reach them. Virgil's versatility was the product of Waitfare's policy of multi-skilling their staff, designed to develop a happier and more flexible workforce and improve customer service. The results were mixed.

"Look where you're going," said Kate. "You nearly demolished that pile of Christmas crackers."

"Sorry," said Hugh, as they entered the next aisle. "This trolley has a mind of its own. Have you seen the biscuits? They've moved everything again."

"Over there, next to the crisps and peanuts. You're not really awake, are you? Too many late nights at the Commission."

"Rather a lot to get done before Christmas. Ginger nuts, I think. Garibaldi are no good for dunking." Hugh turned another corner. "Look. Have you seen Gordon? Over there by the yoghurt. He's got two girls with him. Where does he find them?"

"I'd concentrate on what you're going to cook this evening, if I were you. There's an offer on chicken breasts. Two packs for the price of one. You could use one tonight and put the other in the freezer."

While Hugh was checking sell-by dates Kate glanced in the direction of dairy produce. The smaller of Gordon's companions wore a short fuchsia-coloured skirt. It clashed horribly with her bright red sandals.

"I'll be back from the gym about eight."

"Will Sue be coming back too?" asked Hugh.

"She's going on some blind date. Sounds a bit dodgy to me."

"I hope she'll be careful."

"I'll tell her. If it works out, she might stop ogling the trainers, though I doubt it. She nearly fell off the treadmill last time. Too busy gawping at some bloke's reflection in the mirror."

"While the ice-cool Ms Roberts maintained her reserve."

"Of course. I only have eyes for you."

"And Flash Gordon. Ow! That hurt."

As he wheeled past the light bulbs, Hugh's thoughts turned briefly to Sophie. There was nothing wrong with the odd drink after work, was there?

After supper, Hugh consulted a plant catalogue in the spare room that doubled as a study while Kate checked her e-mail and played a few games of freecell.

"Want to see if you have any messages?"

"Seems unlikely," said Hugh. "Hardly anyone knows my address."

"In that case, I'll play solitaire while you make some more coffee."

"I suppose I could always have a look. Move over." Hugh switched to his account. "Who on earth is Florence de Carmaux?"

"It's not one of those unsolicited ones inviting you to link up with her webcam? Red hot slut; wild, wet and willing."

"What do you know about those? Sorry to have to disappoint you. Good Lord. Listen to this: 'Dear Mr Mullion. Thank you for your message. You must think my silence very impolite. I do apologise for taking so long to reply. I have been away on a long cruise with my husband to celebrate his eightieth birthday and we only arrived home yesterday. I am afraid I do not know the whereabouts of Dorothy Russell or Johnson, as you say she is now. I have not heard of her since the summer of 1946 and that dreadful business about her sister. She completely sank from view. I am sorry I cannot be more help. Kind regards, Florence de Carmaux.' She gives an address in Norfolk. How extraordinary," said Hugh, leaning back in his chair. "Dorothy's never mentioned a sister. Nor has anyone else."

"The plot thickens. Your Dorothy is obviously an axe murderer. I've got this idea. Why don't we forget the coffee and have an early night?"

31

*H*ugh dodged behind the Crime shelves at Toad Books when he spotted the man with the pointed nose approaching the glass door.

"I see you've still got that bird," said the man, banging the door behind him. He unbuttoned his brown raincoat with great deliberation.

"Of course," said Anthony. "Charlie's one of the family."

"Doesn't get any tidier, does it?"

"He. Charlie's a he."

"Albert Schweitzer had an African Grey parrot like that. The bird outlived him by many years. Had an obituary in *The Times*. Have you made a will? You'll need to leave him well provided for."

"Can I help or are you just browsing?" said Anthony, through gritted teeth.

"I was looking for a book about marshes but I don't suppose you've got one," said the man mournfully.

"Any particular book or marsh?" Anthony leaned against the pine table with arms folded. "I can do you an Atlas of the World's Wetlands. Or books on the Marsh Arabs or the Rhone delta. Or do you want something a bit closer to home? Perhaps the Slough of Despond?" he suggested, with just a hint of menace.

"I was after British marshes and their flora and fauna."

"How about Romney Marsh?"

"Sounds better."

"Why don't you try Natural History and Travel and Topography? Then we can review the situation."

"I daresay looking won't do any harm," said the man dolefully. "Had the builders in, have you?"

"Puddleglum is abroad, I see," said Hugh, clutching a brace of green Penguins from the Crime section and a slim book on shade-loving plants from the remainder table. "The damp weather must have brought him out."

"Ssh," said Anthony, putting a finger to his lips. "He'll hear you."

"We're looking forward to the opening of Lucy's exhibition this evening. Her pictures look really good. She's over the moon about it."

"We sent out masses of invitations," said Anthony, "what with the mailing list for her previous Christmas shows plus the names and addresses in her book from the art fair at Battersea plus some people I thought might be interested. Cost a fortune in printing and postage. There's the mulled wine and mince pies too. We'll split all the costs between us. She's got a neighbour…Ken something…to come and play the flute to the assembled company. He'll have to sit out in the bookshop."

But Hugh had stopped listening. He had noticed a girl with long, glossy black hair and a faintly olive skin looking intently at the pictures in the newly painted room through the green doors to the right. She was holding open a small notebook, the gold rings on her fingers catching the light as she wrote.

"Oh, of course," said Anthony, following Hugh's gaze. "She was upstairs when you were looking at the pictures. Come and meet my daughter Caroline. She's over from New York. You'll see her again this evening."

"This is most unexpected," said the man with the pointed nose. He was very nearly cheerful. "Not usual at all. Quite unprecedented, in fact. I will have this one on *Romney Marsh*. And this one on *Pond Life*. And this interesting one on *British Amphibians and Reptiles*. If I may permit myself a joke, Mr Buffo, this is a turn-up for the books. Christmas has come early this year. Does that bird bite?"

32

Come on, Hugh," said Kate, tugging at his elbow. "Practically everyone else has gone. We've said goodnight twice."

"Don't forget, Charlie," said Hugh.

"It's way past his usual bedtime," said Anthony. He was wearing a bright yellow bow tie.

"Goodnight, Charlie."

"Kiss me, Kate; kiss me, Kate; kiss me, Kate," the bird replied.

"Charlie, you're a bad boy," said Anthony. "Why can't you behave?"

It was almost midnight when Hugh and Kate finally exchanged the fug of Toad Books for the clear, cold air outside. The evening had been a great success. The walls of the exhibition space had erupted in a rash of red stickers. Lucy sat exhausted in a corner with a glass of mulled wine and a crumbling mince pie. The familiar streak of magenta in her short black hair had been dyed emerald green to match the sparkly top she was wearing for the launch. Marjorie was in the kitchen with a pile of washing up. Her plum-coloured dress revealed a figure normally disguised by woollens and loose-fitting trousers.

Hugh had spent rather longer than he had wanted trapped in a corner by Nancy Boyes, one of the ladies Lucy taught on a Thursday afternoon.

"You're living in the past," she had said, her skirt caught in a display of gold-sprayed twigs in the fireplace. "You're burying your head in the sand." Nancy was on her fourth glass of mulled wine.

"Not at all. The past is the present and the future too. It's all around us. It's part of what we are and what future generations will be."

"How can the past be the present and the future? That's a contra...a contra...It doesn't make sense." Nancy put a hand on the mantelpiece to steady herself. It was cold to the touch despite the heat of the room.

"Understanding the past can help us understand the present. The past has shaped how we live now and where we live now."

"You just don't like change. You and your Commission thingy want to make sure everything stays the same." Nancy put a hand on Hugh's shoulder. Kate was keeping a close watch from the other side of the room.

"We want to keep the best bits, the buildings and landscapes people value most," said Hugh, gently detaching Nancy's hand. She swayed and looked pallid.

"Anyway, the heritage is big business. Lots of jobs in it."

"At least you know where you are with the past," said Caroline Buffo, passing by with a large oval platter. "It doesn't answer back. That's kinda reassuring, don't you think? Would you guys like a mince pie?"

Hugh and Kate turned into Costard Street by the betting shop at the end of the parade. Their progress was slow but stately. Kate stopped by the pillar box at the point where Costard Street bent and became Dogberry Road. "The wine that was mulled made a Mullion mellow," she declaimed. "So mellow was the Mullion that drank the mulled wine." Kate hiccoughed, giggled and took Hugh's arm.

"What about you then?" he said.

"I'm not a Mullion."

"Perhaps you should be."

"Hugh, you don't mean…?"

"It's an idea."

All the lights were on at number 42. Above the music Hugh thought he heard girls laughing. No wonder Gordon had declined the invitation to Lucy's launch. Kate snatched the keys from Hugh's grasp, pushed open the front gate and strode up the path to their front door. "I'll do the alarm," she said.

33

*H*ugh and Kate got up late the next morning. Hugh was brushing the remains of the almond croissants from the kitchen table when the front door bell rang. He wiped his hands, proceeded down the hall and opened the door.

"Good Lord. Dorothy."

"I can't stay long," she said, breathlessly. "Michael's just going to get some paint mixed at Tints and Hues before he takes me to Waterloo. I thought I'd come over on the off-chance. Michael was lingering in the car down the road in case you were out."

"Come in to the sitting room. This is Kate."

"How nice to meet you at last," said Dorothy. Sorry about my hand. I slipped on your path and hit it against the wall when I tried to stop myself falling."

"That's a nasty bruise," said Kate. You'd better have some arnica." She reappeared with a bottle from the kitchen dresser. "Pop that under your tongue. Don't drink anything for a while. You can keep the bottle. I was going to order some more anyway."

"How kind," said Dorothy. "If I had more time I'd like to hear more about homeopathy. George pooh-poohs it. Says it's just a placebo effect."

"He's not the first, and he won't be the last, but people keep on coming. The diary at the Centre's chock-a-block."

"Sounds like a flourishing practice, if that's the right word. Do you call it a practice, like doctors and vets?"

"That's right. We're wondering about getting another person in to help."

"What brings you to London?" asked Hugh.

"A bit of Christmas shopping and one or two other things. Funny, London's only a couple of hours on the train but it seems like a different world. A nice place to visit but I wouldn't want to live here. Not any more. It's absolutely exhausting. Why do they keep digging up the roads?"

"That's a mystery to us all," said Kate.

"You've been staying with Michael, I take it?"

"Just for a night or two. I wouldn't want to leave George on his own for longer than that. I asked Cheryl Noakes next door to keep a discreet eye on him. She and Tim live in the thatched cottage they've had painted a ghastly shade of pink. She said it was a mistake. I think I may have agreed with her too readily."

Kate suddenly looked wan and left the room. "Excuse me a minute."

"Is she all right? asked Dorothy.

"She's not feeling her brightest and best. Probably too much mulled wine last night, not that she's been well on a few mornings lately. Any progress on the mast front?"

"We got the objections in on time and presented a weighty petition to the council. The next step is lobbying members of the planning committee. They're meeting to decide the application early in the New Year. Cutting it a bit fine, if you ask me.

"The decision isn't delegated to officers, then?"

"They won't let officers decide cases like this. Too controversial. I'm looking forward to the meeting. They give people the chance to speak. I've only got three minutes but I shall make the most of it."

"I'm sure you will. By the way, does the name Florence de Carmaux mean anything to you?"

Dorothy looked blank. "Should it? Is she French?"

"I doubt it, though she may have married a Frenchman. She was a contemporary of yours at St Helen's. I e-mailed her sometime ago when I was still trying to track you down. Her address was on the college website. I can't remember what it said her surname was when she was up."

Kate came back into the room and settled down again.

"You're looking a much better colour," said Dorothy.

"Yes, you are," said Hugh. "Florence de Carmaux only replied a couple of days ago so it was after I last saw you. She'd been away somewhere with her husband. The intriguing thing is that she mentioned that you had, or used to have, a sister. I got the impression something might have happened to her. To your sister, I mean."

"Did she indeed? She has a long memory. A very long memory."

A car horn sounded in the road outside. Through the sitting room window, Hugh recognised Michael at the wheel of his Range Rover.

"Nice to see you both," said Dorothy. "I'll be in touch. Everyone is descending on us for Christmas. Jennifer and Stephen plus Michael and his brood. Look after your davenport, won't you? A good one like that costs a bomb these days."

"I certainly shall. Regards to George. Thank you for the Bramleys."

As Hugh closed the door he saw Michael easing Dorothy slowly into the car. An apple lay by the gate. It must have fallen out of the bag when Dorothy slipped and hit her hand.

"That was a flying visit," said Kate. "She seems quite a nice old thing. A bit evasive, though. I don't think she's as vague as she pretends."

"And not exactly forthcoming about her sister. I wonder what she has to hide. How are you feeling?"

"Not so bad. If we have the pork tonight we can use some of those Bramleys for the apple sauce. Did she forget she'd already given you a bagful?"

34

Dorothy looked through the grille in the door in the wall at the end of the orchard at Bell Cottage. Florence de Carmaux, she thought. Popping up out of the blue after all these years. That she had not expected. Things were beginning to unravel. Why couldn't Colin Smedley have given those books to the Oxfam shop like anyone else? Still, it was too late to turn back the clock. Maybe it was time to lay the ghosts of the past while she still could.

Dorothy ran her forefinger slowly along the edge of the diamond-shaped door handle that she and George had found in a flea market in the Charente many years before. A few gulls floated in the grey sky over the flooded fields. The crenellated tower breaking the line of hills beyond was rich with Gothic conceit and romantic melancholy. It had been completed six months earlier to house equipment to assist the county constabulary in its mobile communications.

"What are you doing out here?" said George. "You'll catch your death."

"Just thinking," said Dorothy quietly.

"You seem preoccupied. You have been since you got back from London."

"There's a lot to do to get ready for Christmas."

"We can always give the holly a miss this year."

"Do you remember Christmases when the kids were young?"

"Of course."

"They always fought over the paper chains. Do children still make those nowadays? And the Chinese lanterns. Like concertinas."

"Why don't you come and have a cup of tea?" said George gently.

"What happened to the chocolate umbrellas? Some were wrapped in green foil, others in red."

"We must have chucked those out years ago."

"And the glass birds that clipped on to the tree. They had tails like overgrown pastry brushes."

"We still have those wrapped up in that box from Marshall and Snelgrove."

"I suppose I'd better make a wreath for the front door."

"We can buy one ready-made in the market."

"It won't be the same."

"But a lot less effort. Come on. Time we went inside."

George led Dorothy slowly towards the house. Mr Tibbs ran after them. While George went into the kitchen to make the tea Dorothy found Hugh's number and picked up the phone.

Part Three

35

Kipling emerged from behind the tree, stretched and made a half-hearted attempt to dislodge the dangling wooden magi with his right paw. Caspar, Melchior and Balthasar spun gently anti-clockwise, clockwise and back again as the thread twisted and untwisted, alternately concealing and revealing gifts of gold, frankincense and myrrh. For presents such as these, Kipling gave not a jot. Something a little fishier was closer to the mark, though a catnip mouse was not to be sniffed at. Or rather, it was, then batted furiously around the hall, trapped in a corner and ritually disembowelled. But such energetic pursuits were not for Kipling on a cosy Boxing Day afternoon. He was heading for the powder blue cushion he knew would be the perfect foil for the ball of ginger fur soon to be upon it. He jumped up, settled down and went fast to sleep.

In his wing chair on one side of the blazing log fire, Hugh woke from his slumbers and looked round blearily.

Kate snoozed contentedly in the chair opposite. Through the French windows he could just make out in the near darkness the cedar of Lebanon in the middle of the lawn. His old swing was still attached to one of the branches after all these years.

In the corner furthest from the fire, Hugh saw his father Henry – like all male Mullions his name began with an H – sitting bolt upright, reading by the light of a standard lamp. He had been impressed by Henry's culinary efforts, produced with military precision on the basis of detailed timetables sellotaped to the doors of the higher kitchen cupboards. Pot-roast pheasant with fennel and puréed parsnips. It was, as the recipe book had said, much juicier and more succulent cooked that way. Not dried up like his mother Muriel's occasional forays into game. The burgundy had been spot on. Perhaps the Christmas pudding was a little on the heavy side but his father had been keen to finish it up and it obviously couldn't be consumed without the madeira that had already made its first appearance in the gravy.

Two years ago, Hugh reflected, his father hadn't been able to boil an egg. He might so easily have passed his days of retirement from the law in morose self-absorption and gloomy introspection. Instead, he had applied himself to cookery, a study of the Incas and the learning of Spanish, in preparation for his forthcoming trip to Cuzco, Machu Picchu and other Peruvian places. His teacher was a woman who had spent many years in Argentina. Her name was not Nina but Fiona, a Scot of some maturity now living with her brother in Sussex.

There was a tacit understanding between Hugh and Henry that Muriel was not to be mentioned. This in no way signalled dislike for the late Mrs Mullion or any desire to expunge her memory. Quite the contrary. It was simply easier that way. Less likely to lead to unmanly displays of emotion, feelings, that kind of thing. But her death had brought Hugh and his father closer and they knew it.

"I can't say I'd like to keep my accounts with a *quipu*," said Henry, looking at the knotted strings in the picture in his book. "I prefer a ledger and a calculator. How about a cup of tea?"

"That would be nice," said Hugh. He rose slowly from his chair, straightened the corner of the rug, and rubbed Kipling gently between his ears. Kate opened her eyes briefly and saw Hugh and Henry standing together. Hugh had his father's slim build and upright bearing.

"What's this about more pictures?" said Henry.

"We succumbed to temptation at an exhibition before Christmas. It was a toss up between *A Street in Bodrum* and *Sunset over Zonguldak.*

"And the winner was?"

"We compromised and bought both."

"I see."

"Lucy Potter – the artist – knocked a bit off," Hugh added hastily.

"You must be running out of wall space."

"I shall do some rearranging. At least Kate's water feature will be outside. Once I've worked out how to put it together."

"She says you're off to Dorset again soon."

"The weekend after next, probably. Dorothy Johnson rang just before Christmas."

"Why are you going?"

"She suggested it."

"Yes, but why are you going?"

"I think she wants to tell me something."

"How long is it you've known her?"

"A couple of months or so."

"Not long. Not everyone your age would want to spend time with an octogenarian. Makes me feel quite youthful."

"We seem to hit it off."

"Kate going too?"

"She's invited and it's not one of her homeopathy weekends. Not sure about the gym."

"All right is she?"

"Who? Kate or Dorothy?"

"Kate. Looking a bit peaky, I thought."

"Just a bit tired. She's been very busy at the Centre recently. All grist to the mill."

"Must be a bit of a worry for her. Income depending on people making appointments. Fine when it's going well but not like a regular salary."

"No, I suppose not."

"Worth remembering. Assam all right for you?"

36

It was a bleak January day. The air felt damp and bitterly cold. The leafless black trees were rocked by the wind. Even the fox that loped across the lane when Hugh pulled up at Bell Cottage looked sullen and dejected. It was not a promising start. But by the time Hugh left Newton FitzPosset that evening his views about identity and the certainty of the past had changed forever. He knew he would remember that day for the rest of his life.

Hugh was well aware what people thought about the Dorothy connection. He did not really care. At first he had enjoyed the challenge and the thrill of the chase as much for their own sake as the remote possibility of finding the other blue book and decoding the message in the note. And they had been a welcome diversion from the boredom of the daily routine. Once he had met Dorothy he had sensed there was more. Even Kate had said as much when Dorothy had paid her flying visit to Dogberry Road.

In truth, this weekend was not particularly convenient for a trip to Dorset and back. But Dorothy had been insistent when she had rung before Christmas, almost imploring. What did she want to say? Hugh had no idea. That was what he had come to find out.

Hugh waited for Dorothy in the study. It was immediately opposite the sitting room but smaller, truncated by the staircase that ran up between study and kitchen. Books made the room seem smaller still. Two walls were lined with them, from floor to ceiling. The other two walls – to the front and to the side – were shared with windows, roller blinds permanently lowered behind the curtains to keep any sun off the books. A small desk with a tooled leather top nestled between a pair of revolving bookcases by the shrouded window at the front. Over the fireplace hung a large picture in the Dutch manner, memorable chiefly for the striped tulips that loomed from an earthenware jug. What little Hugh could see of the walls themselves was a forget-me-not blue.

He inspected the books as best he could, admired the Meissen figures on the mantelpiece, and dibbled surreptitiously in the pot pourri filling the Japanese bowl on the table behind the settee. In a short run of blue volumes with gilt lettering *The Portrait of a Lady* was joined by several other works of the same author. Hugh chose one at random and opened it. There was no inscription, no indication of ownership at all. Just a price,

5/-, pencilled discreetly inside. As he was replacing the book the study door opened with a crash. Dorothy struggled in with a large wooden box, accompanied by Mr Tibbs, his sleek and well-fed appearance belying his protestations of starvation and neglect.

"Let me take that," said Hugh. He put the box on the low table in front of the settee, in line with Dorothy's silent directions.

"Thank you," she said, breathlessly. "It's heavier than I remembered. I had a bit of a job extricating it from the bottom of the wardrobe without waking George. He has a nasty cold and a cough so I sent him to bed. He's sorry to miss you."

"As Kate is you and George. She's feeling a bit under the weather herself but didn't want to stop me coming."

"Just us then. I'd better put this beast out of its misery in the kitchen. Now, Tibbs, will you the beef or will you the pork?" Mr Tibbs protested loudly. "I see. Salmon and tuna it is, then."

Hugh saw that set into the lid of the box was a small brass plate engraved with the initials A.C.R. "My grandfather," explained Dorothy, joining him on the settee. "Algernon Charles Russell." She produced a small key and opened the box. "It's a long time since I looked in here," she said, lifting the lid. "Good heavens. Smell that. Camphor wood." She riffled through letters, postcards, invitations, theatre programmes.

"It's in here somewhere."

She piled everything on the floor and carried on,

unearthing menu cards and sundry ephemera from restaurants and night clubs long gone and long forgotten. A tasselled item caught Hugh's eye.

"The Mirabelle," said Dorothy. "At least that's still there. New Year's Eve 1950-51. Gala Dinner and Dance. That was a good evening. A very good evening. I went with George. And another couple, called Frederick and Frederica, oddly enough. They were always known as the two Freddies. I wonder what happened to them."

"They sound like a musical hall act."

"With loud check suits and brown bowlers. Look at those champagne prices. Sixty-five bob for a Lanson '33. We got through a couple of those. Ah. Here we are."

Dorothy retrieved a large frayed manila envelope from near the bottom of the box. Across the top of the envelope were emblazoned the words: On His Majesty's Service. She tipped some black and white photographs onto her lap and looked through them slowly.

"The Russell sisters. Spot the difference," she said, handing one to Hugh. He saw two little girls in pigtails and summer dresses in the back garden of a largish house. They were laughing and pointing at a black cat in an apple tree. As far as Hugh could tell, the two girls were absolutely identical.

"How extraordinary," he said, sitting up. "Which one is you?"

"The one on the left. I think. This was taken in the garden of my...our grandparents house in Norfolk. Early 1930s, it must have been. About 1932 or '33."

"Like the champagne."

"But maybe not such a good vintage."

"So if you're Dorothy what was your sister's name? I take it she's not still…"

"No. We were Dorothy and Doreen. Alike as two peas in a pod, as you can see. No one could tell us apart. Our parents thought they could but even they got it wrong sometimes. We looked the same, sounded the same, dressed the same. People found it unnerving, unsettling. I think they felt threatened by identical twins. Thought it was unnatural in some way. Of course, we played no end of tricks on people. Not letting on that there were two of us was our favourite. That way one of us could say hello to someone in one place, go off in the opposite direction, and the other could jump out at the unfortunate person further on. Pretending to be each other was another good one. Caused no end of confusion." Dorothy chuckled. She put the photograph back in her lap.

"What about school? Surely people needed to distinguish between you there?"

"At our first school they made us wear different colour ribbons in our hair. Green for Dorothy, blue for Doreen. We swapped them over when we thought no one was looking. The other girls soon caught on to what we were doing and blew the gaff. The school tried badges with our names as well but, of course, they were even easier to exchange. Eventually, our mother was cordially requested to sew our name tapes on the front of our blouses. That presented more of a challenge but we soon became adept quick change artists in the girls' lavatories."

Wind moaned in the chimney. The blinds over the windows moved from side to side. Dorothy carried on.

"My sister and I were very close – in the early years, at any rate. Quite inseparable, except when we were deliberately out to deceive, and even then we were operating in tandem. People tended to shy away from us anyway. We kept ourselves to ourselves more and more, lived in our own little world, hardly saying a word to each other. We didn't need to; we knew what the other one was thinking. Dressing up and making up stories was a logical development, though I don't suppose we looked at it that way then. Started with fairies and princesses and went on from there."

"Didn't it rather limit the parts, being identical?"

"Looking alike doesn't mean being the same, does it? It never did." Hugh was taken aback by the flash of vehemence in Dorothy's voice.

"My sister was the one who had the ideas, took the lead in devising our plays and writing them. We put on plays for our parents. Nothing too complicated but always variations on a theme. Guess who was the king, the great explorer, the knight in shining armour. Not me. Oh, no. My sister made sure she was noticed and got the praise. I always felt she was more favoured. I doubt that she was really but it seemed like it at the time and that's what matters. Hard to think of me as a shrinking violet now, isn't it?" There was a glint in Dorothy's eyes.

"Well…" Hugh smiled complicitously.

"I was very shy as a child but acting in our plays helped me overcome it, even playing second fiddle to my sister. I was both hiding and showing off, if you like. In a funny sort of way, it was only by being someone else that I could overcome the barriers to being myself. Trite perhaps, but true. I don't want to exaggerate, though. It was only really within the family circle that the differences between my sister and me were apparent, as far as I can tell, and then only when we were together. Outside, we presented a united front."

"That's what first got you interested in acting?"

"I suppose so but there was more to it than that. Even at an early age I liked words, lifting them from the page and making them come alive. You can only appreciate the sound and rhythm of language when you hear it out loud. Saying it in your head isn't the same. And half the fun is in the interpretation, making something different of the same material. My father was a big help there. He made us learn poetry and Shakespeare speeches by heart and recite them to visiting friends and relatives. I used to practise with Wilfred."

"Wilfred?"

"My rabbit. Toy rabbit, that is, as in Pip, Squeak and Wilfred. We used to read their adventures in the *Daily Mirror* when we were children. Wilfred is my lifelong companion. Rather quiet but a good listener. He's been a great comfort to me over the years. I still have him upstairs."

"I have a bear like that but he's a mere stripling by comparison."

"Take good care of him and he will of you. Mind you, I've had some close shaves with Wilfred. He went missing several times when we went away to school. Hidden under the mattress, flung around the dorm with lacrosse sticks, thrown out of the window, all manner of indignities."

"You were at boarding school, then?"

"At St Cecilia's in Somerset. Michael's Alice is down to go there. Music is still its forté, I believe. I imagine she will find the school very different from my day. Our day. For a start, Michael says they now have a headmaster. Quite unthinkable then. There was only one master in the place and even that was considered very daring. He taught maths or physics. Maybe both. All those adoring females to contend with. Must have been pretty intimidating for him, actually. Julian something. Faraday. That's it. Julian Faraday. I heard that he was killed over France later. What a waste." Dorothy sighed.

"So you had a headmistress with an Eton crop sporting a monocle. Or a scaly old dragon breathing fire."

"Think of Miss Trunchbull on speed, only worse. Letitia Tank was her name. Dreadful woman. Four foot ten inches high and much the same wide. She had the loudest voice I have ever heard. All the staff were terrified of her. She addressed them by their surnames. The pupils, too. She used to thunder down the tiled corridors, making random inspections of the knickers with a malacca cane. Woe betide those wearing non-regulation pairs. 'By their knickers shall ye know them,' she bellowed at my friend Beatrice Cheese. 'We do not wear grey serge at St Cecilia's. Go and change them at once and take one hundred lines.' They should have been navy blue, in case you're wondering."

"She'd be arrested nowadays," said Hugh.

"I do hope so. Miss Tank had a thing about crossed legs too. She roamed round Chapel and Hall looking for them. If she spotted her quarry she wacked the poor girl on the knees with her cane."

"Unbelievable."

"Crossed legs were inconsistent with the standards of propriety expected of a St Cecilia's girl, Miss Tank informed us. She'd have a fit if she knew that they had dances with the boys' school now and joint productions of the school plays. Hadfield was strictly out-of-bounds when we were there. Miss Tank was a rabid man-hater."

"Makes you wonder how Julian Faraday got in – or why he wanted to, for that matter."

"They probably couldn't find a woman to teach maths or physics at the time. I must say that the standard of teaching was pretty awful in those days. Most of the staff were OCs…"

"OCs?"

"Old Cecilians…with barely a qualification between them. Miss Muffler's idea of teaching the geography of the United States was to make us learn all the states and their capitals by heart. That was it. Came in handy with the GIs a few years later, though. They were most impressed."

"Didn't the war change things?" said Hugh, shifting to the left and draping his arm over a large tapestry cushion.

"Not fundamentally," said Dorothy. "We stayed where we were, unlike some boarding schools. The grounds and buildings remained virtually intact, though the railings did go for scrap. We took in girls from one or two other schools. Put them up on camp beds in the gym. The regime relaxed a bit after they arrived and even more when the redoubtable Miss Cakebread replaced Miss Tank in 1940. I don't know how Miss Tank would have coped when clothes rationing came in. The traditional uniform went for a burton. We lost the tuck shop too."

"Destroyed by enemy action?"

"No. There weren't any bombs anywhere near the school. The tuck shop was used as a British Restaurant for people in the town. The place reeked of mince. Not that there was much to sell by then. By that stage it was raw carrots for a penny a time."

"I hope you did your bit for the War Effort."

"We used to go off on our bicycles and help the farmers remove charlock from the fields. Pernicious and invasive weeds, they were. Couch grass too. And some of the school grounds were turned into allotments. More wretched carrots. We helped with the digging. We stayed at school during the holidays to avoid the bombing in London. Not that there was any at first. We missed our parents dreadfully."

*

Hugh found himself increasingly drawn into Dorothy's story. He was happy enough to listen, even if he did wonder where it was leading. He sensed that she was going over ground she hadn't covered for years, dredging up episodes long forgotten or suppressed. He had known about a sister, of course, from Florence de Carmaux, but what was the 'dreadful business' she had mentioned? Was that what Dorothy wanted to say or was there something else?

"How were things with your sister?"

"We both began to be fed up with being so much in each other's pockets and being mistaken for each other. The amusement value wore off as we got older. We made half-hearted attempts to go around together less and develop our own circles of friends but it never really worked. A few of the younger girls latched on to us. They liked nothing better than to make our beds and fill our hot water bottles. I strongly suspect my sister was behind the abduction of Wilfred. He was found wearing a gas mask on top of the art cupboard. It was much too big for him but then I never had one that fitted properly myself. Just as well gas masks were never needed."

"Were you both still acting?"

"My sister took to producing the House plays – *Androcles and the Lion*, *The Rose and the Ring*, and so on. She stopped acting entirely, except when we did *Twelfth Night*. Our house mistress prevailed upon her to play Sebastian to my Viola. Luckily, we didn't attempt

The Comedy of Errors. With two sets of twins there'd have been no escape. My final appearance was as Tony Lumpkin in *She Stoops*. He must be one of the most irritating characters in the whole of British drama. My sister made me do him in a ludicrous rustic accent that nobody could understand. This is a photograph of me playing him here."

Hugh leaned forward and studied the photograph of a girl swamped by a loose frock coat and wearing an ill-fitting wig. She was quite unrecognisable as Dorothy.

"What about Oxford? Did you both go there?"

"We were heading in that direction. Both pretty bright, actually. Sailed through School Cert and all that. We were expected to go to St Helen's in due course to read English. The school had some sort of connection with the college. But when the time came I couldn't face it." Dorothy paused. "Being with my sister was like seeing myself constantly in the mirror, with all my imperfections reflected back at me. No one really treated us as individuals. More like two halves of the same person, which in a way we were, I suppose. I can't say I blame them since we'd spent so much time pretending to be each other. But I just wanted to be me, without being very sure there was a me to be. Or, if there were, quite what it was. Going off to Oxford together just held the prospect of perpetuating the same old problems and feeling under my sister's thumb. I daresay Oxford would have been less claustrophobic than St Cecilia's but I decided that it wasn't for me."

"What?" said Hugh, sitting bolt upright. "You weren't at Oxford after all?"

"No," said Dorothy calmly. "I flunked the exams, as people say these days. Deliberately, of course. My parents were angry and bewildered and the school was none too happy. My sister, of course, was cock-a-hoop, on the outside anyway."

"But why did you say you were at Oxford? George thinks you went there, doesn't he?"

"He does, yes."

Hugh thought back to Dorothy's prevarication about the OUDS on his first visit to Bell Cottage.

"So why on earth…?"

"It's not quite that simple. Believe me."

"Yes, but…"

"This is hard enough without the third degree."

Hugh sat back, trying to hide his frustration.

"So what *did* you do?"

"I joined the Ministry of Public Safety and National Resources." Dorothy made it sound the most natural thing in the world.

"Good Lord. What as?"

"A sort of secretary cum clerk."

"I can't quite see you as a civil servant. You didn't seem ecstatic about Michael becoming one. I thought you were the arch-enemy of bureaucracy."

"And so I am but this was wartime. A lot of people became civil servants during the war. State control grew enormously. There were masses of restrictions and regulations but they were largely accepted as a necessary evil. Not that there was much choice. On the other hand, I always thought that fining our neighbour, Mrs Twigg, for feeding the birds in her garden was going a bit far."

"Fined for feeding the birds?" said Hugh in wide-eyed disbelief.

"It was judged to be wasting food. It was only a few scraps."

"Extraordinary."

"Perhaps not quite so extraordinary when you consider the shortages. People nowadays have no idea. But even so."

Dorothy put the envelope and photographs next to the box on the table, eased herself up slowly and walked stiffly towards the fireplace. She stretched and remained standing for a moment with a hand resting gently on the mantelpiece before taking to the pale yellow armchair diagonally opposite Hugh. He spread towards the remainder of the settee.

"Coming back to London after St Cecilia's must have been a jolt," said Hugh.

"It was. Some places I'd known had completely disappeared. Bombed out of existence. Some streets were in ruins. Rubble and willowherb, as the poet said. But then others were completely untouched and looked no different. It was the randomness of it all… . In some ways I found the half-destroyed buildings more upsetting than those that were completely flattened. Seeing people's houses blown open, exposing what little they had to public gaze. Intrusive."

"Meanwhile, your sister was in Oxford."

"Not at first. Until she went up she was at home. She helped my mother with her WVS work and did some fire-watching too."

"I thought it was the WRVS."

"The R was added much later. Sometime in the sixties. My mother broke her ankle in the blackout, not long after the war started. Tripped over something in the dark and then couldn't find her own front door. The ankle never was right afterwards."

"And your father?"

"Too old to fight, thank goodness. He was in publishing, wrestling with paper shortages, but did his bit as an air raid warden. He was a dab hand in the garden too. Dug up all our nice herbaceous borders and planted cabbages and things."

"Carrots?"

"Yes. More bloody carrots, pardon my French. There was no escape from the curse of Doctor Carrot and Potato Pete. But at least we had flowers on the roof of the Anderson shelter. The nasturtiums lasted for months."

"How was life at the Ministry?" asked Hugh.

"Long cold passages and hot stuffy little offices," Dorothy said quickly, almost as if she had the answer prepared. "The Ministry had taken over the headquarters of an insurance firm evacuated to darkest Buckingham-shire. They were forever creating new offices out of plywood to cope with reorganisations and expansions. One day a corridor was there, the next it had disap-peared. Turned into more offices. Most disconcerting."

"What did you do?"

"I spent my days dealing with bumf and typing minutes and notes of meetings. Endless meetings at which nothing much was decided. And I made the tea, of course. It tasted like liquid cardboard. Looked like it too. I had to lock everything away at the end of the day. Otherwise it vanished overnight, especially the teaspoons. I was in a division called Promotion of Domestic Economy B."

"B?" said Hugh. "What did that stand for?"

"It didn't. It just distinguished us from A and C. The head of the division was a charming and cultivated man – not a career civil servant – but my first boss was a nasty piece of work. He didn't like women at the best of times but especially not young women who were cleverer than he was. He took pleasure in finding fault and passing off my ideas as his own. Fortunately, a doodlebug got him before I did." There was a note of triumph in Dorothy's voice.

"Seems a little drastic."

"You didn't work for him. He had a particular thing about paper, economy in the use of. There were posters everywhere saying 'Don't Waste Paper'. He insisted on going through our wastepaper baskets to check that every square inch of paper had been used before it was collected for recycling, as we would say now. If he found a blank space he would whoop with delight and chastise the unfortunate basket owner in front of everyone else. When he caught me out once he informed the entire office that I was squandering scarce resources and undermining the War Effort. I suggested that we took down his posters and wrote on the back of those. He was not amused."

"What an awful man. What was he called?"

"Howard Thrift, appropriately enough. He kept a close watch on typewriter ribbons too. We had to use them so often that the typing was virtually illegible. Same with the carbon paper. He abolished margins – 'top, bottom and both sides, Miss Russell'. And there was big trouble if we failed to use single spacing for drafts. I had an ally in another girl, Vera Tate. He berated her for making a necklace out of treasury tags when she was bored one day."

"Rather scratchy," said Hugh.

"She wasn't going to wear it. He made her stay behind to unpick it."

"Is this how we won the war?"

"We had a few better things to do. I was given responsibility for the new Sub-Committee on Providence and Frugality. SC (PF), it was called."

"A sub-committee of what?"

"The Advisory Committee on Domestic Economy."

"Don't tell me: ACDE."

"Right first time. HT was rather annoyed that a mere female clerk was to look after the sub-committee."

"Sounds rather unusual."

"It was, but our head of division, Rex Laidlaw, had noticed some work I'd done on a pamphlet we'd issued: *Prudence in the Home: Handy Hints for the Busy Housewife*. He was chair of the new sub-committee and he asked me to be secretary. There was a last-minute panic about the agenda for the second meeting. I could only think of one item to put on it. 'Then you can't call it the agenda,' said the abominable Thrift. 'Agenda are things to be done. If there's only one, it's an agendum. Have you forgotten your Latin? RL won't like it one bit.' That was the extent of his contribution. The problem solved itself once I'd added minutes of the first meeting and matters arising."

"You got on all right with Rex Laidlaw, I take it?"

"Like a house on fire. I particularly liked his silk pyjamas. Cherry red with cream piping. I imagine he bought them before the war."

"Er…"

"No, no. Nothing like that. There was some flap on," explained Dorothy, "which meant he had to stay too late to go home. He slept in the office. People did from time to time so they needed to be prepared. Vera and I saw Rex emerging from the bathroom the following morning. He must have got up later than he intended."

"Tell me about Vera," said Hugh.

Dorothy shifted in her chair. She cleared her throat. "A rather different background, if you know what I mean. She knew a thing or two about life, not to say men. A real eye-opener for me. She thought I was very young and naïve, which indeed I was. She couldn't believe we'd been going round the town in crocodiles at St Cecilia's right until the time we left. She introduced me to pubs, and things took off from there."

"I thought people read and listened to the radio."

"People read voraciously and I was no exception. New books were snapped up in no time. Having a father in publishing helped, of course. The classics were even harder to get but fortunately we had most of those at home already. My mother paid frequent visits to the local library and to Boots…"

"The chemists?"

"You could borrow books from their Booklovers Library. You must have come across books with the green Boots stickers on the front cover."

"I'm not sure I have. What about Penguins? Did you leave your Penguin at a post office for members of the Forces when you'd read it? That's what people were told to do, wasn't it? I picked up some tatty wartime Penguins in a charity shop before Christmas."

"Quite right. Yes, I did. I was less of a fan of the wireless − except for ITMA, of course. *It's That Man Again*. Tommy Handley. A must on a Thursday night. We all thought it was an absolute hoot then. It seems painfully unfunny whenever I hear a bit repeated now."

"So you propped up the bar of your local."

"Heavens no. Vera and I went all over the place, making sure we caught the last tube home. Stepping over all those people on the platforms. Talk about vile bodies. I can still remember the smell." Dorothy wrinkled her nose. "The pubs were a refuge from the drab and gloomy world outside. Nice and warm and welcoming but very crowded and smoky. People smoked like chimneys. Cigarettes were never rationed but they were often in short supply. I didn't smoke myself but Vera would do anything for a packet of Woodbines."

"Any regular haunts?"

Dorothy warmed to the theme. "Our favourite was a pub near Oxford Street. The Spotted Dog. It was mock Tudor – half-timbered and leaded lights. Had wood panelling inside and bright red lino. The pub was very loud and fights were always breaking out. But it was all great fun. You never knew who you were going to meet or whether you'd ever see them again. Here today and gone tomorrow. People lived for the present. When the beer ran out we went somewhere else."

"Putting back pints doesn't seem quite your thing," said Hugh.

"I usually stuck to halves. I'm not really a beer person but wine and spirits were harder to get, though there was some North African stuff around at some point. Very rough. Quite undrinkable. Oh, and I did once try some pastis in a pub in Old Compton Street. Made me feel very sophisticated."

"Did you go everywhere with Vera?"

"For a lot of the time but we weren't alone for long. A couple of servicemen on leave and we soon became a foursome. Of course, they were often looking for a bit more than company."

"Romance in the blackout."

"More like grappling in doorways for the most part. Double British Summer Time was a damned nuisance sometimes. Fine for farmers but not much good if you want to be furtive with a man in uniform."

"Ah, the good old British Tommy."

"Well, I wouldn't say that." Dorothy looked coy. "Goodness didn't really enter into it. Vera and I played the field. London was a pretty cosmopolitan place, full of foreign soldiers and sailors and so on. They seemed very dashing to us. Made the English seem rather staid by comparison. The Poles were notoriously lecherous but I particularly liked the Free French sailors." Dorothy's face lit up. "Lovely little berets and red pompoms."

"What happened to the innocent young girl from St Cecilia's?"

"She grew up and had a whale of a time."

"Love among the ruins."

"Let's go and have some tea in the kitchen."

While Dorothy was making the tea Hugh counted the blue and white banded storage jars on the shelves of the large pine dresser. Each bore letters denoting its intended contents: Demerara sugar, icing sugar, ground ginger, gravy salt, baking powder…

"Seventy-three," said Dorothy matter-of-factly. "By no means a full set. I had a flour jar but that got broken, thanks to Mr Tibbs, so now I keep flour in the lump sugar." Dorothy put two mugs of tea on the table. One mug was marked Cyanide in gold, the other Strychnine. "Where were we?" said Dorothy, as she and Hugh sat down.

"Liaising with our allies. What about the GIs you mentioned earlier?"

"I went to dances with the GIs. I'd hardly ever been

to one before. Restaurants too. The Americans seemed to have so much money. Taxis everywhere and nylons galore. Goodbye gravy browning and eyebrow pencil." Dorothy lowered her head as she struggled to remember some names. "Joe Stetson," she said slowly, looking up and smiling at the recollection. "From Bismark, North Dakota. He taught me the jitterbug. Tom Bowler from Great Falls, Montana. Pretty free with the Lucky Strike. I gave them to Vera. And then there was Arthur Jones." She hesitated. "He was a black man."

"Not too common in Britain then, I imagine."

"No. One restaurant we went to refused to serve him. Caused a bit of a stir. That was pretty unusual though. In my experience, most British people got on very well with the black GIs. It was the white GIs who objected to them. There were some nasty incidents. Arthur Jones insisted on meeting my parents. My father was rather uncomfortable about it at first but my mother was much taken with him. He looked just like Paul Robeson. As he was going, he presented my father with a packet of razor blades and my mother with some scented soap and a banana. We shared it after he had gone."

"A banana," said Hugh, with a mixture of pity and incredulity.

"We hadn't seen one for ages," Dorothy protested, "let alone eaten one. Vera won a lemon once. A great rarity. It was first prize in the office raffle. Onions were quite often given as prizes too."

Hugh suppressed further comment and thought of

the array of fruit and vegetables in Waitfare at any time of the year.

"It was the GIs who first got me interested in jazz. They began to thin out in the run-up to the Normandy landings but I did get to see poor old Glenn Miller at the Plaza with Bill Jackson. Must have been about July 1944."

"You seem to have had a good war. No time for any acting, I suppose?"

"Once or twice. The Touchstone Players put on a few things at the local literary institute and were crying out for help. My parents came to see me as Lydia Bennett in a dramatisation of *Pride and Prejudice*. We all went to J B Priestley's *Dangerous Corner*. The siren went off in the middle but everyone stayed put and carried on."

"Meanwhile, your sister was well away from it all in Oxford."

"I went to see her a few times, in spite of everything. She was rather jealous of the time I was having in London. It took an age to get to Oxford during the war. Private motoring was completely out by that stage, not that I could drive anyway. I didn't take my test till 1960. Trains were slow and crowded and dreadfully uncomfortable. They kept stopping in the middle of nowhere for no apparent reason. Reading staved off the boredom."

"And people talked to each other?"

"That's one of my abiding memories of the war. Talking to strangers. People I'd never dreamed of speaking to before. Not just on trains but in shops, in queues, on buses, all over the place. Do you know, until war broke out we'd hardly ever spoken to our neighbours, let alone been into their houses? I suppose we all felt we were in it together. There were all sorts of strange conversations to and from Oxford. I remember once that a girl was so delighted to get a letter from her fiancé in the army that she read it out to the entire compartment and told us her life story. The odd thing was that she'd seen him quite by chance in a newsreel at the cinema only the night before. Just for a few seconds. Another time, a man pressed me into a corner and droned on *ad nauseam* about Proust, which I hadn't then read. As he was getting off the train at Reading he turned round and said I reminded him of Veronica Lake. Nonsense, of course, even with my hair as it was then."

Hugh smiled. "How was Oxford compared to London?"

"Deathly quiet. There was hardly any traffic and even the bells were silent. But there was still plenty of evidence of the war. People in uniform all round the place, evacuees and so on. Strange little huddles of East Europeans speaking incomprehensible tongues. Refugees, I suppose. I remember seeing jeeps and tanks along St Giles too. St Helen's had been taken over as a military hospital. There were huts all over the college gardens and on the tennis courts."

"What happened to the girls?"

"They were in houses scattered all round north Oxford. A large old vicarage served as the college base.

That's where they had their meals. St Helen's proper was closed to undergraduates, except for the library, I believe. My sister was in a house just off the Woodstock Road. The girl in the next room was called Polly Mitchell. She became quite a well known MP. Chaired a select committee for years. I often saw her on television."

"Not the one who smoked a cigar and swore like a trooper?"

"That's the one. Hard to imagine it, isn't it? She looked so delicate in those days, like a porcelain figure. How people change – on the outside, anyway." Dorothy sighed and took a sip of tea. "My sister and I once went out with Polly and had a lentil curry for the princely sum of ninepence at the Taj Mahal. We were joined by a friend of Polly's called Lawrence Humphries. We saw him speaking at the Union once. Had to watch from the balcony upstairs. It was all very tame. No one dared to criticise the government or the conduct of the war. I wonder what happened to him."

"Another casualty?"

"I never heard. Mind you, men were something of a rarity in Oxford at that time. Undergraduates, anyway. My sister used to target solitary males in Blackwell's. She'd feign an intense interest in obscure volumes nearby in the hope of catching their eye and procuring an invitation to coffee somewhere. She spoke highly of the coffee and buns at Ellistons."

"Your sister had some luck, then?"

"Oh, yes. She developed an attachment to a history don at St Luke's. He was married but hadn't seen his wife since she went off with their children to Canada in 1940. I forget the name of the boat. I met him once with my sister outside the Classic Cinema in Walton Street. He was most disconcerted to see two of us, especially as we were dressed almost exactly the same. I was rather annoyed. I'd turned up in Oxford in a floral blouse my mother had made from some old curtains she'd found in a box in the loft. My sister, if you please, was wearing one in the identical material."

"How bizarre. Rather creepy." Hugh took a long swig of tea.

"Things were a little tense between us at the tea party in her room that afternoon, not helped by jocular references to Tweedledum and Tweedledee. My sister wasn't in the best of humour anyway. She had got up early and queued in the rain for cakes and buns at the cake factory in Summertown. Polly brought in one of those wind-up gramophones and we listened to *The Flight of the Bumblebee* over and over again. The men had to be out by six and my sister took to her bed with some Friar's Balsam and the pink hot water bottle my mother had bought at Timothy White's while we were still at school. I had one the same. I went off to the Mitre with Polly and her brother who was visiting her on leave."

"It all sounds a lot safer than stumbling through the black-out in London."

"Oxford was blacked out too for a time. I must say that Oxford in the black-out in the light of the full moon is one of the most haunting things I have ever seen. I shall never forget it. But I think most of the girls did feel guilty about studying in the middle of a war. Arguing whether C S Lewis or Lord David Cecil is the better lecturer does seem a bit removed from everyday life on the Home Front. On the other hand, people did have war work to do."

"Really? What sort of work?"

"My sister used to cycle up to Headington Hill to dig the allotments. She did some fire-watching at the Bodleian too. Had to sleep there on a camp bed. Ruth – she had the room next door to my sister – helped delouse the heads of evacuee children. Polly was a waitress in the Red Cross Club in Beaumont Street and she helped to show GIs round Oxford."

"Ah, the GIs again."

"The place was full of them. Some of them were extremely persistent. My sister was offered large sums in exchange for her virtue. I believe she finally succumbed after a dance at the town hall, which she certainly shouldn't have been at. She pushed her bicycle all the way home to north Oxford."

"Coming back to London in the vacations must have been a shock for her."

"A lot of the girls stayed up and helped with the war effort in and around Oxford. My sister did a stint on a farm. I'm not sure she was technically a land girl but it was that sort of thing. She regaled us with unpleasant stories of rat-catching by the hay ricks at threshing time. Had string round the bottom of her trousers so the rats couldn't run up. More tea?"

Dorothy stood up creakily and took the two mugs in the direction of the kettle. There was a momentary flash as their gold lettering caught the light. Hugh was reminded of Caroline Buffo's rings gleaming under the spots in the white room at Toad Books. Mr Tibbs twitched involuntarily as he lay curled up in a box by the central heating boiler. Hugh's chair wobbled gently on the uneven stone floor as he wriggled to get comfortable.

"Your sister was presumably still at Oxford after the war," he said when Dorothy had sat down with the tea.

"Until the summer of the following year. While I was in the throng at Buckingham Palace on VE Day shouting for the King my sister was alleged to have been dancing the conga down Cornmarket and jumping through a bonfire at Carfax. I only went to Oxford once or twice after the war ended. What a difference when the servicemen started to come back! They seemed so much older. The boys straight from school didn't stand much of a chance."

"St Helen's moved back to its proper home, I take it."

"Almost immediately," said Dorothy. "My sister's room was bleak and poky compared to the one she'd had before and the whole place smelled like a hospital. My last experience of Oxford at that time was in June 1946. We cycled out to the Perch in the afternoon and in the evening went to see the OUDS' production of *A Winter's Tale* in Exeter gardens. I think they still called themselves the Friends of the OUDS then. Polly was there with a younger girl called Florence Baker. She was a friend of one of the production team, Nigel de Carmaux. She disappeared into the shadows with him after the performance. I never saw her again, though I heard later that they were married."

"So you did know who Florence de Carmaux was," said Hugh with more than a hint of good-natured accusation.

"I'm sorry about that. A minor dissimulation. I wasn't ready to spill the beans. Perhaps I should get in touch with her."

Not the first dissimulation, it seems, thought Hugh. You did have a sister and you didn't go to Oxford. You took a drastic step to avoiding being with her and then kept going to see her. Clear as mud. Where are we? 1946. Wasn't that when Florence de Carmaux said something happened?

"What did your sister do when she left?"

"She came home to stay before she was due to start training as a teacher. I had left the Ministry by this time and was working as an assistant to the Director of an oil company. My mother was delighted to have both of us back together but my sister and I were beginning to get on each other's nerves again. I spent as much time as I could out of the house and was beginning to think of getting a flat of my own. Just rented but I could afford it with the pay I was getting by then. My mother was busying herself with preparations for our joint twenty-first birthday party at the beginning of

August. It was to be at our grandparents' house in Norfolk."

"Was it a big party?"

"Lots of people were invited. The family itself was thin on the ground – both my parents were only children and my father's parents were long gone – but my mother unearthed vast numbers of alleged friends of the family who were supposed to have known us since the year dot and had survived the war unscathed. My sister and I invited our own friends so there were two quite distinct age groups. Then, of course, there were our grandparents. Another generation again. They seemed terribly ancient and doddery. In fact, they must have been younger than I am now. I expect I seem ancient and doddery to you…"

"On the contrary…" But actually, thought Hugh, she *is* looking more fragile. More vulnerable somehow. He couldn't quite put his finger on it.

"Young people never stop to think that older ones have been their age once and weren't born decrepit. Still, I'm sure I was just the same," said Dorothy. "My grandparents – they were Bagshawes not Russells – seemed rather fazed by the prospect of the hordes due to descend on them but my mother assured them she had everything under control. Mrs Partridge and her daughter from the village were detailed to help with the refreshments, though there was still rationing, of course. Hodgkin had the garden looking perfect. I still remember the magnificent display of phlox."

"Why did everyone have to trek up to Norfolk?"

"It was a large house and garden, reasonably accessible by train and I don't think my grandparents would have made the journey to London. A good place for a party and it had a swimming pool too. Not in the best of states but a pool all the same. Everyone was told to bring swimming things but it was mostly the younger ones who did. I spotted Dick, the gardener's boy, peering at us over the wall. He reminded me of Mr Chad."

"How did it go?"

Dorothy paused. "The party itself was a great success," she said deliberately. "In the evening there was dancing to music provided by my friends the Wild Wooders. Just a small band of amateur musicians I met through the Touchstone Players, and a singer called Georgina. She was a cousin of the clarinet player." Dorothy stopped for a moment. "Around midnight my sister came up to me and suggested a dip in the pool. I assumed she had invited others too but it turned out to be just the two of us. We got changed in the summerhouse and picked our way across to the pool. It was dark and what moon there was kept being obscured by passing clouds so it was hard to see what we were doing. My sister was bragging about her degree – a first, of course – which one of our godparents had chosen to make much of in his speech earlier on. He said he was sure I would make a first-class secretary too."

"Very morale-boosting."

"Quite. As she was getting into the pool my sister slipped and hit her head on the side. At least, that seems to have been what happened. I was focused more on getting in myself. It was all so quick. She didn't really scream. It was more a yelp of surprise. And then she went under. I could make out the top of her head in the water – we both wore white bathing caps. When I got there she wasn't moving at all, just bobbing face down in the middle of the pool. I tried to keep her head out of the water and pull her to the side but it was awkward on my own. I cried for help over and over again. The band had started up so no one in the house could hear me. All I could see were lights through the trees and people moving, dancing behind glass. It was just a blur. Eventually I got to the side and managed to drag my sister out. I tried to resuscitate her but there was no response. I left her lying by the pool and went to get help. I remember the torches flashing and the sound of running feet. But it was too late. She was dead. Drowned."

"How awful. But the note: 'Fear death by drowning'. It *was* an accident, wasn't it? Not that I'm suggesting…"

"Oh, yes. She slipped and fell. And we had had a certain amount to drink. Even so, perhaps I could have made more of an effort to try to pull her out and run to get help sooner than I did. The note was a bizarre coincidence. It was a bit of a game between us. Sending each other notes with lines from poems or plays, sometimes books. We'd been doing it on and off for years. One of us chose a line from something without saying where it was from. The other had to identify the next line. This time it was my sister's turn to start. She had sent me a note a few days earlier with a line from *The Waste Land*: 'I do not find the Hanged Man'. It was under Wilfred's right arm." The ghost of a smile crossed Dorothy's wan face. "I just returned the compliment with the next line of the poem. I slipped it under her hairbrush. When she drowned I panicked and tried to find the note when I got back to our room. I couldn't. There was no sign of it anywhere. She must have put the note in the Henry James at the time and it stayed there until you found it. I've never read the book myself."

"The writing in the note and the book are the same – and in the theatre books you gave to Hermione Smedley."

"They are," said Dorothy, "but the hands are different. My sister's writing and mine were identical."

"I don't understand why the book has your name in it if it was your sister who went to St Helen's. Why should she write your name?"

"She didn't. She wrote her own."

"But you're Dorothy Russell...Johnson."

"She is Dorothy Russell. Or was then. I was Doreen."

"What? Why on earth did you swap names?"

"Not just names," Dorothy said quietly. "We swapped identities too – only this time it was *my* initiative and she couldn't answer back. When I ran to get help I realised that no one could tell by looking which one of us had drowned. The differences while we were both alive were more of personality, only really noticeable when we were together and only then to our parents and one or two others. I decided to say that it was

Doreen who had been in the pool. Doreen the mere secretary not Dorothy with the first-class degree from Oxford. It gave me the chance to reinvent myself with the education and chances I deserved and could have had."

"Just like that, on a whim?"

"It was too good an opportunity to miss. Makes me seem rather cold and calculating, doesn't it? That's not how it was, though. I just blurted it out in a split second. No doubt it helped the story that I had inadvertently picked up Dorothy's towel instead of my own in the dark. It had her name on it."

"Surely your parents at least must have realised you weren't the real Dorothy. You can't change personality at the drop of a hat."

"No one would have expected me…Dorothy…to behave normally in the circumstances. Everyone was upset and was not exactly surprised that I was too. If I was subdued and withdrawn in the days that followed, that was par for the course, wasn't it?"

"But you didn't do what your sister was going to do and train to be a teacher."

"No. When it came to it I realised that I couldn't quite pull it off. Having the brains is one thing but I couldn't suddenly acquire three years of knowledge and experience, her friends, their expectations, and so on."

"She'd have left Oxford behind, met new people, moved on. Started a new phase of her life. And you knew something of Oxford and her friends anyway."

"It's easy to say that sitting here now. That's not how

it seemed to a frightened girl well over half a century ago. I didn't know what to do. I couldn't go forward as Dorothy and I couldn't go back to being Doreen. I'd burned my boats."

"So what did you do?"

"I flipped, cracked up. Or pretended to. It seemed the best way to wipe the slate clean and lose the baggage of my sister's past. By far my most challenging role to date. I don't suppose it was remotely authentic but it seemed to convince people I'd had some sort of breakdown brought on by my sister's death. A specific and identifiable cause. All the more understandable as we were twins and identical ones at that. Everyone was very nice about it, teacher training was deferred and rest and recuperation were the order of the day. After much humming and ha-ing, the experts declared that there was no fundamental clinical problem. The odd visit to a particularly gruesome Victorian institution persuaded me not to carry things too far."

"At least you'd bought time to think what to do next."

"I sat around and read a great deal. I made a start on Henry James but never got past *The Golden Bowl*. I did a few things in the garden that my father was still trying to restore to its pre-war glory. He never did remove the Anderson shelter. I even helped my mother at the WVS. I don't think voluntary work is really my thing. I need something more to get my teeth into."

"What of Dorothy's…your sister's…friends? Didn't they come and see you?"

"At first, yes, but they became increasingly caught up in their own new lives and gradually they tailed off. Polly was pretty good. Oh, and I had a most unexpected visit from Miss Muffler. Call me Mildred, she said. I couldn't bring myself to do it. It seemed unnatural after all those years at school. She sat down with a cup of tea and tested me on American state capitals. I was doing fine until we got to Idaho. I always have had difficulty with that one."

"Boise," said Hugh.

"Well done. I think this calls for a florentine or would you prefer a macaroon?" Dorothy brought to the table a round tin purporting to contain a selection of Danish biscuits. She removed the lid with a clatter. "Vera Tate – the girl from the Ministry – came to see me once or twice too. Vera had been at the party. She found the situation difficult to handle. I looked just like her friend Doreen and yet…I nearly let the guard slip but pulled myself together just in time. I lost touch with her too. The conditions that had brought Vera and Doreen together had changed completely and I couldn't admit to all the things we had done anyway. We might just as well have been strangers."

"When did you decide what to do?"

"One thing I was clear about early on was that I didn't want to go into teaching. Quite a few of my sister's contemporaries at St Helen's went that way but I didn't relish the prospect of going back to school in any capacity. I saw an advertisement in the local paper for an assistant in an antique shop not far from where we lived. Red Anchor Antiques. I'd been in there several times with my mother. It was run by an extraordinary old boy called Kelvin McInnes. He sported a smoking cap and a tartan waistcoat. Had a small Scottie dog that snuffled contentedly around the place. I always thought I'd trip over it carrying something priceless but I never did. I took the job on a temporary basis and somehow weeks passed into months and months into years."

"So that's what set you down the antiques trail," said Hugh, wiping chocolate from his fingers. He had chosen the florentine.

"Yes, and when I started to acquire some nice bits too. I bought a number of things for my parents and subsequently inherited them. At least there wasn't that ghastly business of dividing the estate. I don't envy Michael and Jennifer. The corner cupboard in the study was one thing I picked up. The card table in the hall was another. The Saxton map of Norfolk by the stairs I originally gave to my grandparents."

"I thought furniture and maps were more George's line."

"They are but I didn't know him then. My real interest is china and glass but my tastes were more catholic when I was starting out. There was a lot to learn. I was quite content in my little niche though I had a bit of a scare after I'd been there a few months."

"What happened?"

"A chap came in to ask about a Staffordshire lion in the window and suddenly said he knew me. Insisted that we'd met at a production of *Measure for Measure* in Christ Church cloisters in 1944. I didn't have the foggiest who he was. He kept going on about it. You can't have forgotten Richard Burton's Angelo, he said. I said: yes, of course, how silly of me, or something like that, and hoped he'd go. He did eventually – with the lion – but not before he had proceeded to tell me a lot about himself. He asked nothing about me, fortunately. I've met a number of men like that."

"But not George."

"Oh no." Dorothy unwound and sat back. "No, no. George was quite different. A kind and gentle man. My rod and staff. He's been a great support to me over the years and he's had a lot to put up with. He's as tough as old boots but he can keep his light hidden under a bushel. When I first met him I wasn't sure there was anything under his bushel at all."

"The determination of a quiet man. Not to be underestimated."

Dorothy smiled. "Quite so."

"He told me you were members of the same amateur dramatic society. Did he say the Mummers?"

"That's right. They used a hall in Twickenham. It must have been about 1948...1949...something like that. I was already a member. I had my own flat by then. He was poached from another society when our regular stage designer ran off with the wife of the lighting man. George didn't just design the sets. He did most of the construction too and could turn his hand to stage management and what have you. Remarkably versatile.

All I could do was act, though I did drift into props in later years."

"So George was saying."

"Oh, did he? It became clear after a while that George's interest in the theatre went well beyond the practical side. He knew a lot about plays, from Greek drama on. Eventually, he plucked up courage to suggest we saw something at the Arts Theatre Club in Great Newport Street. I can't for the life of me remember what it was. We often went to their monthly club suppers. We never looked back. I used to meet him after work. Sometimes theatre, sometimes ballet, but usually theatre. On other occasions he'd come in my direction and we'd go to Richmond or Kew. It was nice being with someone whose reactions to plays were very much in accord with my own. We were both very fond of the poor old St James's Theatre, near where George worked."

"I don't think I know it."

"Before your time, I fear. It was demolished in 1957. A great shame – but at least George managed to rescue some of the finger plates. They're on the sitting room doors. It was the failure of the campaign to save the St James's that made me think about standing up and fighting for things locally. We were in Surrey by this time, of course. I shall never forget Laurence Olivier and Vivien Leigh in *Anthony and Cleopatra* – or was it *Caesar and Cleopatra*?" Dorothy paused. "Actually, it was both. May 1951."

"Festival of Britain year," said Hugh.

"That was fun, while it lasted. It seemed so colourful and lively after all that post-war drabness."

" 'A Tonic for the Nation', didn't they call it?"

"That was it. George used to catch the special bus service from Clapham Common, not far from where he was living by that time. It brought him to the Festival Pleasure Gardens in Battersea Park. I met him by the Dance Pavilion and off we'd go." Dorothy's feet tapped the flagstone under her chair. "There's a picture somewhere of George and me on a fairground horse. He was wearing a trilby. Looked like Dick Barton. I'd been rendered speechless by a Sharp's toffee. Teeth completely stuck together. I couldn't say anything for ages. George said something about savouring the moment but wouldn't explain what he meant." Hugh smiled but did not enlighten her.

"You got married later that year, I think George said."

"No. George proposed to me towards the end of the year and we got married the following one. He was as nervous as a kitten. I don't know what took him so long. I thought I'd made it pretty obvious but there we are. Even then, I couldn't imagine life without him. I don't mean just the plays and things but in other ways too. He made himself useful, then indispensable. Decorated my flat, made new curtains, re-upholstered some chairs. Once, when I'd been away for a night at an antique fair in Sussex, I came back to find two window boxes on my sills. They were painted dark green, I remember, and full of geraniums: red, pink and white." Dorothy's face lit up at the memory. Her eyes moistened.

Neither spoke, then Hugh said softly: "George had made them?"

Dorothy nodded. "And brought them all the way from Clapham on the tube. Not the contents. I think he got those round the corner. I used to water the plants using a jam jar before he got me a small watering can. Once I put so much water in George said I'd drown them. I collapsed in sobs on his shoulder."

Dorothy dabbed at the corners of her eyes with the sleeve of her lavender silk shirt. "Sorry to be so silly," she said.

Hugh's first thought was to comfort her, to put a reassuring hand on hers. But he hesitated too long and the moment passed. "How much does George know?"

"He knows I had a sister who died in a drowning accident and that we were identical twins. He probably saw photographs of the two of us years ago at my parents' house."

"Did he know your sister's name?"

"Yes. That's to say he thinks it was Doreen. I've never told anyone what really happened. You've no idea what a relief it is to talk to someone after all these years. You'll keep it under your hat, won't you?"

"Of course. I won't tell a soul but why didn't you say anything to George?"

"How could I tell him that I was really someone else? And what would have been the point anyway? What purpose would it have served?"

"You wouldn't have had to carry the burden for all these years. What's in a name? I can't see that it would have made any difference to George. You'd still have been the person he married."

"Would I? A liar, a fraud, an impostor? It's not a risk I was prepared to take."

"But why are you telling me all this? You've only known me for a couple of months."

"Seems longer, doesn't it?" Dorothy faltered. "I just needed to tell someone while I still could. You seemed right. I can't really explain why."

"While you still could?"

"I'm not exactly in the first flush. You don't mind, do you?"

"Not at all." Hugh felt rather flattered – but more than that. The shared secret created a sense of complicity, cemented a bond between them.

"There is just something else," said Dorothy. "When my sister died she was pregnant. She had told me a couple of days earlier and sworn me to secrecy. It all came out later, of course, except that by then people thought it was me, if you see what I mean. Some very unpleasant things were said about my wartime liaisons, most of which were perfectly innocent, as it happens. It was like eavesdropping on a private conversation. When my sister first told me I assumed it was one of those Italian ex-POWs she'd first met during her stint on the farm in Oxfordshire. Quite a few stayed on after the war and I knew she'd continued to see one or two. But no. I was wrong. It turned out to be a man who'd been a Major in the Intelligence Corps. He had come back to Oxford after the war to take his degree but my sister didn't meet him until shortly before she left. His name, she said, was Terence Johnson."

"You don't mean…?"

"When I met George I made no connection. Johnson isn't exactly an uncommon name and, to be honest, I'd forgotten all about Terence. I'd never met him or anyone who knew him."

"But didn't he try to get in touch with you at the time?"

"No, not a word. Some years later I found out why. Shortly before we were married George said he'd had a brother whose time at Oxford had overlapped with mine."

"A major in the Intelligence Corps called Terence."

"Yes. He'd been killed in a car crash on his way to a party in Norfolk. He was just going to see a friend from Oxford, he'd said. He hadn't told his family about my sister and my family didn't know about him."

"So he and your sister and the baby died on the same day. How awful."

"Dreadful. George showed me a photograph of the two of them taken just before the war. They were uncannily similar."

"Not twins, surely?"

"No, but very similar all the same. Terence was a few years older than George."

"How extraordinary."

"At first sight," said Dorothy, "but maybe no more of a coincidence than those stories of identical twins you hear about. You know the sort of thing: twins separated at birth and years later turn out to be doing the same jobs, married people looking the same and with the same name, called their children the same thing, and so on. Still, it makes you wonder if we're in control of anything, doesn't it? It all seems inevitable, mapped out…"

"Except that, in this case, fate intervened so that only one couple came through."

"I suppose so. Not a happy story," said Dorothy forlornly. "Sometimes I'm not sure whether it's more tragic to die or to go on living. There hasn't been a single day since my sister drowned that I haven't thought of her. That's a lot of days. I try to keep myself busy."

As Hugh was preparing to leave, Dorothy said, "Just a minute. I have a little something for you. No, not apples. And a couple of other things as well." She reappeared with a carrier bag in which tissue paper and bubble wrap were much in evidence. "Open them when you get home."

In a lay-by somewhere in Dorset Hugh carefully unwrapped the largest item. It was a glass goblet engraved with fronds of fern and two words: *Remember Me*.

37

---

*T*he following Sunday morning Hugh opened the front
door to Anthony Buffo, paying a rare visit to number
40. Instinctively, Anthony started looking at the books
and pictures before he sat down on the new settee. Kate
said it was dark blue; Hugh insisted that it was indigo.
Anthony lingered in front of two paintings by Lucy
Potter until Hugh coughed politely.

"Dorothy wanted me to give you this." He handed
Anthony a pink lustre mug from which a frog appeared
to be making frantic attempts to escape. "It's a Sunderland
frog mug, according to the note that was with it. She says
sorry it isn't a toad but hopes it will be the next best thing.
The frog looks quite cheerful considering its predicament."

"It's very nice," said Anthony, turning the mug round
slowly, "but why? I've never even met her."

"I think it's her way of saying thank you. I found
the blue book in your shop. That set me down the
Dorothy trail."

"And you helped to locate Colin Smedley," Kate put in quietly.

"Even so."

"Look what she gave me." Kate removed from the mantelpiece a small silver rattle.

"What's this bit for?" asked Anthony. "Looks like coral."

"I think it's for teething," said Hugh. "More for ornament than use these days, I daresay." He glanced at the large glass goblet sitting in the window, coldly elegant in the grey January light.

"I'll write to her," said Anthony. "I've just come from Lucy's. She's feeling a bit overwhelmed. The exhibition has been a great success. Lots of visitors – and they buy books too! Charlie's very pleased with all the attention. I've had several inquiries about use of the space. If things take off it could be a nice little side-line. Suky Sims is booked for February."

"She of the small white chapels amid the olive groves."

"The very same. And I'm trying to get Jill Mantis for the following month. She does unusual things with bits of driftwood. I'll advertise these properly in the art mags and see how it goes. It'll be like old times."

"Will it? In what way?" said Hugh.

"My wife and I ran a gallery in South Kensington a number of years ago. The Romulus Gallery. The name was Martha's idea. She's American. We first met in Rome and she said the name would be a permanent reminder of our meeting. Rather ironic, as things turned out."

"What did you go in for? Paintings? Sculpture?"

"We sold paintings, prints and drawings. We had a bit of publicity when someone broke in and helped themselves to some lithographs by Matisse and Bonnard. Martha took most of the stock with her to New York but I hung onto a few things myself."

"Including some Picasso etchings."

"Correct." Anthony beamed.

"You didn't go in for books in those days?"

"I did some of buying and selling from home. The odd catalogue and a bit of book search but the gallery was the main thing then. The business was going well until Martha met a dealer from New York and decided that she'd like to set up with him, in every sense. To cut a long story short, we separated and she and Caroline stepped westward. It was all fairly amicable in the circumstances."

"Is that why you go to New York?"

"I see Caroline and keep an eye on the gallery. It's in SoHo – off Broome Street, if you're ever there. The New Romulus Gallery, no less. After the dust had settled I became a director. I take things over from time to time. Gavels produces the occasional find – but not often. Most of the stuff is deadly dull. I like your *Church in a Wooded Landscape*, though. It rings a small bell. Maybe I saw it at the viewing without registering it."

"Hang on," said Hugh, going into the hall. He returned with the picture and gave it Anthony, face down. "I believe it's what they call a respectable provenance."

" 'The Romulus Gallery, South Kensington'," read

Anthony. "I do believe I typed this label myself. What a small world."

"I'm sorry we didn't have a chance to speak to Caroline properly," said Hugh. "Her mince pies were much in demand."

"She went back with a bag full of small paintings Lucy had in her studio. They're selling like hot cakes, apparently, so I've been instructed to bring out more. The trouble is, there aren't any more to speak of and I'm due to fly out again in a few weeks. So Lucy's going into purdah until she's churned out another batch."

"You must miss your daughter," said Kate softly.

38

*H*ugh and Kate were curled up on the settee when the telephone rang.

"It's Anthony. Put the News on quick. I've just seen the headlines. Looks like La Dame aux Mobile Phone Masts has made it to the small screen." Hugh lunged at the remote control and stabbed a button, not a moment too soon.

"Over now to Nigel Noggin outside the district council offices in Okeminster. Sounds pretty lively, Nigel."

"It certainly is, Kevin. People are saying there's been nothing like it in this small Dorset town since Okeminster Wanderers won the Cup in 1922. Councillors are meeting here this evening to decide the fate of the proposed mobile phone mast on, or rather in, the steeple of the Church of St John's. This controversial proposal has cut the community in two and triggered a hate campaign against St John's vicar Oliver Primrose. Earlier this evening the chanting crowds you see waving placards behind me parted like the Red Sea to let through the protesters' leader Dorothy Johnson. She was accompanied by CAMM chiefs Len Spinks and Lilly Pond…"

"Remind us about CAMM, Nigel."

"The Campaign Against Mast Madness, Kevin. They help local people up and down the country fight mast proposals. A few moments ago Dorothy Johnson was addressing the packed planning committee meeting. Here are her closing words:"

"In conclusion, Mr Chairman, I call upon the committee to stand up for the health of every man, woman and child in this town of ours. What is at stake is the future welfare of people living and working and going to school in Okeminster. We have heard much of the alleged benefits of mobile phones, of obscure guidelines that don't even address the community's concerns, of the bland assurances of the government and mobile phone operators. I say remember BSE, remember thalidomide, remember asbestos. Don't treat the people of our town as human guinea pigs. Don't take the risk. Put people before profit and reject the mast proposal."

"Well, Nigel, that was quite a performance."

"It certainly was, Kevin. And we've just heard that the committee have voted unanimously to turn down the mast against their own officers' advice. Here comes Dorothy Johnson now."

"I can hardly hear you above the noise, Nigel."

"Well, Dorothy, that was stirring stuff. You must be very pleased."

"I'm delighted. Not for myself. I am an old woman whose day is nearly done. But for the people of Okeminster and for the future. This is a victory for humanity, decency and commonsense. We can all take pride in that."

"I'm joined now by Alick Smart, Public Affairs Manager of mobile phone operator Tfourtwo, previously known as Sunray. You must be very disappointed by the committee's decision."

"I am indeed. This decision was based purely on rhetoric and emotion. It flies in the face of government guidance and the huge public demand for mobile phone technology. We shall certainly appeal. We live to fight another day."

"Sounds like we haven't heard the last of this. Thank you both. Now back to you in the studio, Kevin."

"Wow," said Kate. "That was quite something. Did you see the way the light caught Dorothy's hair? It was almost like a halo."

39

Hugh was looking through the window at the snowdrops sheltering at the foot of the jasmine. The dull sky overhead was a menacing shade of pewter, lightening gradually towards the west to the merest suggestion of pale apricot. A lone magpie perched on the trellis above the fence dividing the back garden of number 40 from that of number 42, Gordon's house. They had not seen Gordon for a while.

"What are you doing? You've been standing there for ages," said Kate.

"Just thinking," he said.

"You've been in a funny mood ever since you came back from Dorothy's."

"It was rather a marathon session. I felt completely drained."

"Sounds like you got her life story. I liked the bit about the toffee at the Festival of Britain. My mother must have been about four or five then."

"Hm," said Hugh, sketching abstractedly with his fingernail in the condensation on the window pane.

"What was that you said about a wreath?"

"Oh," he said, half turning towards Kate. "On the front door. Wired on to the knocker. It came from the market in Okeminster, apparently. She said it was the first time in fifty-odd years she hadn't made one herself. It seemed to upset her."

"Old people always find it depressing not to be able to do the things they used to do. Would you like some tea?"

"Hm. Please." Hugh went over for the umpteenth time Dorothy's account of the accident and its aftermath. "Perhaps I could have made more of an effort to try to pull her out and run to get help sooner than I did." Was it really an accident? And, even if it was, did she see an opportunity to get her own back on her sister rather sooner than she said? Maybe, maybe not. It hardly mattered after all these years. Perhaps frantic activity – the stage, her causes – was just her way of coping with…what? Guilt? Loss? Loneliness? Hugh thought back to the vase standing by itself at the auction viewing, to the isolated urn in the garden at Newton FitzPosset, both separated from their other halves. Effective in their own way but lacking somehow. A pair was more than the sum of its parts, after all.

Who was it had said you know where you are with the past? Oh yes. It was Caroline Buffo at Lucy's launch party. She was wrong. There was no certainty or reliability about the past. It was shifting and insubstantial. Hardly a secure foundation for the present. What was history but selective reporting?

At least Dorothy had got things off her chest. But she had lived a lie for sixty years. Once she had started she couldn't stop. O what a tangled web we weave! It was difficult to believe that George suspected nothing. Had she never let the mask slip in all that time? George knew there had been a twin sister, supposedly Doreen, who had met her death by drowning. What had he thought when he saw the note, apparently in Dorothy's writing? He had said the only D he knew was Dorothy. True in that he had never known Doreen. Perhaps George read nothing into the note but, as Dorothy said, he played his cards close to his chest.

Why had she chosen to reveal her secret to him, Hugh Mullion, someone she hardly knew? "You seemed right," she had said. Whatever that meant. He supposed she must have trusted him. Feeling comfortable with someone was more important than how long you'd known them. But the initial sense of flattery and complicity in a secret shared had begun to wear off. Dorothy's burden had become his burden. In his bleaker moments, he just felt used. She had told him her story for her own benefit, not his. What would she have done if Kate had come with him? Or if George had been around, for that matter? Idle speculation. One thing *was* certain, though. He would not betray Dorothy's confidence.

"Come and sit down," said Kate, bringing in the tea. "I got you some mini chocolate chip muffins."

"I feel better already."

"Tell me again about the rabbit and the gas mask."

40

_____

*W*hen Hugh arrived at Power People, Sue was already there. He found her warming up on a bicycle. She was half-watching, on the television screen high up on the wall ahead of her, the repeat of a gardening programme made up of the best bits of previous gardening programmes. The commentary was inaudible above the musak blasting from strategically placed loudspeakers. Hugh found the rhythm distressingly infectious. He adjusted the seat on the bicycle next to Sue, put his towel on the handlebars, set the controls and started pedalling.

"Nice to see that the art of topiary is alive and kicking," said Hugh, glancing at the screen. "How are you then?"

"Still in a state of shock," Sue whimpered. "I woke up this morning and found this bloke beside me in the bed. He was covered in tattoos. Had them everywhere. And I do mean everywhere."

"Even on his..?"

"Yes."

Hugh gulped and muttered something about a colourful character.

"Makes Kate's swallow-tail look pretty tame," said Sue. "Is it her left shoulder or her right? I can never remember."

"Her right. What on earth were you doing last night to end up with an illustrated man in your bed?"

"I went to a club in Brixton with Margie from work. Called the G Spot. It's quite hard to find but worth it when you do. I must have got totally pissed. I don't know what happened to her. She didn't turn up this morning. I sent her a text but haven't heard anything. I hope she's all right."

"Aren't you getting a bit old for clubbing, if you don't mind my saying so?"

"I do wonder sometimes. Most of the people at these places look about seventeen but you never know your luck. Which reminds me. Who was that gorgeous girl I saw you with on Thursday night, in Regent Street?"

"Thursday, you say. Regent Street. Let me see," Hugh said slowly. He appeared to be giving the matter careful consideration. "Oh yes. That must have been Sophie Bradshaw. She's a television researcher, doing a programme on the future of historic buildings and landscapes. I was pointing her in the right direction. Giving her information, contacts, that sort of thing. Purely in the line of business."

"Hm. Sure about that, are you? You haven't been indulging in a bit of the extra curricular, I hope."

"Good heavens, no." Hugh paused. "No, I haven't." He paused again but kept pedalling. "I've known her for a while. I can't say I wasn't tempted…I don't think I'd be much good at that sort of thing. Everything would get so complicated, wouldn't it? There aren't enough hours in the day. I'm not that organised. It's strictly serial monogamy as far as I'm concerned and that means Kate, just Kate."

Sophie had made Hugh think more carefully about what he really wanted. As had the arrival of Gordon West on the scene. Perhaps he had been jealous, a bit. Sophie and Gordon had in fact brought Hugh and Kate closer together. Of course, Hugh had never mentioned Sophie to Kate, had he? It seemed better to leave it that way. Water under the bridge. Let's hope Sue wouldn't blow the gaffe.

"Still," he said. "You never know who you're going to meet, do you?"

Sue said nothing for a while. Then, softly, almost a whisper: "No. You don't." She got off the bicycle, wiped down the handlebars and took a slurp from her bottle of water. "When is it that Kate's having her scan?"

Hugh perked up. "We went to Queens this morning. Saw Professor Marinatos himself."

"Why didn't you tell me?" Sue squealed. "Is it a boy or a girl?"

"Girl. Two girls. It's twins."

"That's fantastic. I'm so excited," said Sue, hugging

Hugh tightly. A woman with muscular arms, pink hair and a Tintin quiff looked up from the lat press. "You must be over the moon."

"I'm still reeling from the shock. Between you and me, I'm quietly delighted."

"I'll give Kate a ring. How's she taken to the prospect of double trouble?"

"Her usual practical self. Immediately started talking about double buggies and not blocking the aisles at Waitfare. We'll probably have to think about a bigger house but I don't want to tempt fate."

"Shame after all you've done to the house and garden."

"Not that much really. Somewhere bigger will give me…us…more scope. More room for books too."

41

*H*ugh and Kate turned right out of Costard Street –
the sign lately rendered Custard Street by a local wag
– and walked along the parade. It was a cold, grey
February morning. Spiro from the Mini-market was rearranging pink grapefruit before turning his attention
to the sweet potatoes. Kate let go of Hugh's arm and
unwound her stripy scarf before preceding him into
the shop next door.

"We were just admiring the sign, Marjorie," said Kate.
"Very smart."

"Toad Books and Gallery. It does have a certain ring,"
said Hugh.

"Sounds rather grand, doesn't it?" said Marjorie. "I'm
so pleased about your news."

The bookcase beyond the green door to the left
had been removed. In its place stood a pine cupboard.
On the top a percolator steamed contentedly, flanked
by the paraphernalia of coffee making and consump-

tion. The smell of freshly brewed coffee pervaded the shop.

"Can I offer you a cup?" inquired Marjorie. Hugh and Kate declined. "I spend half my time washing up these days. Anthony insisted on proper cups and saucers. Spoons too. He wouldn't hear of plastic cups and stirrers. Said it would lower the tone."

"He has a point," said Hugh. "And you'd need a bin for the used ones."

"When I'm not washing up, I'm making more coffee or checking the milk and sugar. You wouldn't believe the arguments we had about those." Marjorie ran through the debate about the milk: skimmed, semi-skimmed or whole milk? Should the milk be in small cartons, in which case what would they be put in and did they want the empties left lying around? Or should the milk be put in jugs, in which case wouldn't it go off out here and wouldn't people spill it anyway? Then there was the sugar: brown or white, sachets, lumps or loose? What if people wanted sweeteners instead? Marjorie felt the need to talk.

"It all seems to have been resolved," said Kate, glancing at the insulated jugs of milk and the basket full of sachets.

"War nearly broke out when that Peter from next door came in with the cupboard. 'Coffee?' he said. 'I'd have had tea, myself. I never say no to an orange dazzler.' I had to put my foot down."

"Where *is* Anthony?" asked Hugh.

"He's popped out. For five minutes, he said. That was half an hour ago."

"Things have certainly taken off," said Kate. "Aegean chapels seem to be attracting a lot of interest." Through the green doors to the right she could see people milling around the bright white room, holding cups of coffee and peering at the pictures.

"Reminds them of their holidays," said Marjorie. "Mind you, most of them come in for the free coffee, if you ask me. I told him to charge for it but he wouldn't."

"The books have gone from the remainder table," said Hugh.

"I'm reorganising," said Anthony, walking in with a large bag of parrot mix. "Shunting a whole load of stuff upstairs. Never a dull moment at Toad Books."

"And Gallery," said Hugh and Kate in unison.

"You noticed. I need to decide what goes upstairs and what stays down here. I'm tempted to give the boot to Food and Drink."

"Got a lychee?" said Charlie, from the summit of his open cage.

Hugh and Kate walked slowly down the rest of the parade towards the high street. Destination Waitfare. Kate had the shopping list in her pocket. Hugh said he had invited people round to supper that evening; Kate said that she had invited them to a dinner party. Opinion was divided on whether that made the slightest difference to what people were going to wear and whether it mattered anyway. Outside the dry cleaners they were greeted effusively by Peter Gubbins. "I must dash," he said. "I've left my friend Tom up a ladder with a barometer. I do hope he hasn't dropped it." As Peter made off, he turned and said, "You will call one of your girls Jemima, won't you? Like my car."

"I wonder how Sue will get on with Gordon," said Kate, as they crossed Fortinbras Road, on the corner by Bin Ends.

"Get off, more likely, knowing Sue," said Hugh. "Gordon's no slouch, either."

"That was uncalled for."

"You sound just like your mother."

Kate did not rise to the bait. "Brave of you to invite Roger and Mrs Roger. What *is* her name?"

"Anne. I don't have to worry too much about the Rogers now. He goes at the end of the month."

"Director of the... .What is it?"

"Joint Forum for the Urban and Rural Built Environment," said Hugh, walking round the wheelless bicycle chained to the lamp post.

"How did he take to your getting his job?"

"Seemed fine. Positively enthusiastic. I'm sure he knew before I did."

"You didn't have long to wait after the interview."

"There were only two other candidates. I kept having to avoid the Chief Executive's eye when I passed her in the corridor. Now she beams at me."

"You'll have a bigger office."

"And some different roofs to stare at."

"Hugh Mullion: Director of Conservation Policy. I like it. I quite like him sometimes too."

"You're not so bad yourself."

Hugh and Kate crossed the high street and passed through the automatic doors of Waitfare. They were confronted by an enormous display of Easter eggs where once there had been pot plants and cut flowers.

"They've moved everything again," said Hugh, looking round for a trolley.

42

The following Saturday, Hugh was unpacking shopping while Kate recovered at the kitchen table with a cup of coffee and a chocolate orange. The doorbell rang as he was putting the milk in the fridge. He went into the hall and opened the front door.

"Good heavens. Michael. Come in."

"I can't stay long. Just passing through. We're off to look at an art exhibition in a bookshop near here. Jane's in the car reading a draft report her team have produced about improving management of the interface between something and something else." Hugh closed the door behind him. "I'm afraid I've got some bad news." Michael sounded business-like. "My mother died on Wednesday."

Hugh paused. He put a hand on the dado rail. "I am sorry. How could she? I mean... . She looked so well. Robust. Indestructible." But he recalled that Dorothy *had* looked frailer the last time he had seen her.

"Who is it?" called Kate.

"I'll be with you in a minute."

"She hadn't really been well for sometime," said Michael, "but she carried on regardless. We told her to slow down – but she wouldn't. She was driven somehow, had the energy of a woman half her age. Well, seemed to have."

"How's George coping?"

"He's pretty dazed. They were together over fifty years. My sister Jennifer's staying with him. I was down there yesterday. It's strangely quiet without my mother there. Almost as if the life has gone out of the house too. The cats keep wandering around looking for her."

"Will George stay there by himself?"

"Jennifer suggested he come to live with her and Stephen but he can't stand the thought of living in a small house in London with nothing much to do. He says leaving Newton FitzPosset with all its memories is the last thing he wants. He's got the garden and his workshop and the people he knows in the area but I wonder whether he'll have the will to keep going. You know what often happens in long-standing couples when one of them dies. He's older than my mother is…was."

"I expect the neighbours will keep an eye on him."

"They've already been very good. The local paper wants to do an article on my mother for next week's issue. Jennifer and I were trying to piece things together with my father last night. The first few years after she left Oxford were a bit of a puzzle."

"A long time ago now."

"As you say, a long time ago. I don't suppose we'll ever know, not that it really matters. It's only a few years in a long life."

"When's the funeral?"

"End of next week. I'll phone you with the details."

"Not at St John's, I take it?"

"The vicar did offer. Forgive and forget, he said, but my father was clear that my mother wouldn't have wanted it held there. It'll be at St Mary's in the village."

The bell rang again. Hugh opened the door.

"I don't think you've met Jane," said Michael of the woman in black who stood framed in the doorway.

"How do you do," said Hugh to the fair-haired woman he had previously seen at Gavels' auction some months before. A look of recognition flashed between them.

"Nice to meet you," said Jane, glancing quickly at a picture on the wall above Hugh's left shoulder: *Church in a wooded landscape*. For another £10 it might have been hers. "You left this in the car, Michael."

He extracted from the battered carrier bag two blue volumes with gilt lettering.

"My father wanted me to give these to you. They belonged to my mother. I believe you found one of them. I'm not sure which."

"The second one. Volume II."

"So you completed the story, then."

"In a manner of speaking." Hugh had completed the portraits of two ladies, just as Sue had said, with uncanny prescience, when he had embarked upon this quest. "I'll see you next week. I hope Kate will come too. She never managed to get to Newton FitzPosset while Dorothy was alive."

"That would be good. You and Kate must come round for a drink sometime."

Later that evening, while Kate was upstairs, Hugh took the two blue volumes off the davenport and knelt with them on the carpet. He flicked through them; nothing fell out. He wondered what Dorothy had done with the note. Both volumes had the same inscription on the flyleaf, written precisely in blue-black ink. So Volume I had turned up in south London after all, if not in quite the way he had anticipated. Perhaps he had better read *The Portrait of a Lady* while there was still some peace and quiet.

As Hugh replaced the books on the davenport he noticed that the second drawer down on his side was very slightly open. He took hold of the two neatly turned wooden knobs and gently pulled the drawer towards him. He found inside a small illustrated edition of *The Rubáiyát of Omar Khayyám*, some of his mother's diaries, and a quantity of photographs. They were mostly black and white but a few were in colour. Hugh looked through them slowly. Near the bottom of the pile he found a picture of his mother holding a small baby. It must have been taken over thirty years before.

"Is that you?" said Kate, coming quietly into the room before he could close the drawer. "Pity I only knew your mother when she was grey. That flaming red hair looks rather magnificent. It's just like Dorothy's, isn't it?"

43

I'm shattered," said Kate, collapsing on the settee at 40 Dogberry Road.

"You were asleep almost all the way back from the funeral. I'm glad we spent last night in Okeminster," said Hugh. "At least I didn't have to drive to the far side of Dorset and back in a day."

"The woman at the hotel seemed to remember you."

"Olive Snook. She told me about Dorothy's mast campaign when I was there before. Dorothy mentioned her name when she rang me at the pub next door, the White Hart."

"How did Olive Snook know I'd changed the colour of my hair? I've never met her before."

"I've no idea. Perhaps she thought you were somebody else. Drink?"

"Please."

Hugh left the room hastily before Kate could probe

further and returned with a bottle of red wine and two glasses.

"Good turn-out," said Kate. "The church was packed."

"The flowers at the crematorium were impressive, weren't they?" said Hugh, handing her a glass of wine and taking a sip from the other himself. "Did you see that one of the wreaths was from Colin Smedley. There was one from the Fairview Players too. It was supposed to be family and close friends but George insisted I went – and you too, of course."

"But you were close to Dorothy."

"I suppose I was, yes. Silly, really." Hugh joined Kate on the settee. "I only knew her for about three months."

"Seems longer. You learned a lot about her."

"Michael said she was worried that George would go first but I think she knew she was going to die."

"How do you know that?"

"Just a feeling," said Hugh. "I think that's why she invited me...us...down that last time. She was saying goodbye, had I but known it." He thought back to that afternoon a few weeks earlier. "I just needed to tell someone while I still could," she had said. "I'm not exactly in the first flush." Hugh looked at the glass goblet in the bay window, catching the light from the standard lamp: *Remember Me*.

" 'I am an old woman whose day is nearly done'," said Kate reflectively.

"What?"

"It's what Dorothy said in that television interview. Her last public performance. She's at peace now anyway."

"Let's hope so. Michael's eulogy was good. Struck exactly the right note. Rather unexpected. I think I may have misjudged him."

"You were getting on well with his wife afterwards."

"Jane, yes. She likes books and pictures. Turns out that she knows Toad Books…"

"and Gallery…"

"…quite well. She thinks Anthony is a bit difficult. Funny our paths have never crossed there. I wonder why she wasn't wearing black."

"I was stuck with Jennifer's Stephen," said Kate. "He kept going on about inter-operability and improved functionality. What is it about people in computers?"

"Apparently, he and Jennifer may move in with George. She's trying for a job at Okeminster School and he can work from anywhere, as long as it's wired up or whatever you call it."

"At least George wouldn't be on his own at Bell Cottage. He seemed to be coping well, all things considered."

"Remarkably animated," said Hugh, draining his glass and pouring another. Kate had hardly touched hers. "It must have been a trial for him. He was a bit apprehensive about Jennifer and Stephen going to live there. He finds her didacticism a little relentless. It doesn't stop at the school gate."

"I liked George. He told me how Bell Cottage got its name."

"I always assumed it was because of that bell over the garage."

"The cottage and Bell Lane took their names from the pub. The Demented Ox."

"The *Startled* Ox," said Hugh.

"Whatever. It used to be called the Bell, until the brewery sold it a few years ago."

"Like O'Malleys. Is nowhere safe?"

"George was closeted with one woman for ages."

"The one who looked like Margaret Rutherford as Madame Arcati? That was Florence de Carmaux. She sent me the e-mail from Norfolk. She said that Dorothy had been in touch and they were due to meet. She produced some photographs of Dorothy in her Oxford days. I wouldn't have known it was her at all."

"It's going back a long way, before she even knew George. How long were they married?"

"Over fifty years. In fifty years' time you'll be the same age as Dorothy and I'll be the same age as George."

"Do you think we'll still be together in fifty years?" said Kate.

"I'm banking on it."

"Our children will be middle-aged."

"I think it's about time I made an honest woman of you, don't you?"

"Kate Mullion, eh? I accept – on one condition."

"What's that?"

"You make me a chocolate spread and peanut butter sandwich."

"No wonder you feel sick."

44

*T*he following afternoon, Hugh stood by the window staring into the back garden as the light began to fade. Kate had her arm around his waist and her head on his shoulder. The blue tits in the crab apple tree darted about as they always did. Raindrops lingered on the wallflowers beneath. The wistful notes of 'Summertime' penetrated the gathering gloom.

Hugh sighed. "It's hardly a summer evening on Catfish Row, is it?"